VO.

David M. Staniforth

Text copyright © David Staniforth 2016

This is a work of fiction. Names, characters, places, incidents and dialogues are products of the author's imagination or are used fictionally. Any resemblance to actual people, living or dead, events or locales is entirely coincidental.

170216

Acknowledgements

Over the course of writing and publishing books I have encountered a great many people that I need to thank. Were I to do so, it would be a small book in and of itself. Therein: a generic thank you to anyone not mentioned here, whether it be for the support I've received or for a review you have kindly bestowed in appreciation of my writing.

I do have to make a special mention, however, of a group of people who have been kind enough to give up their time to read preliminary drafts of this book, who have lent me their support and helped me to iron out creases in the text. They are: Kath Middleton, Christine Terrell, Jean Coldwell, Katy Jenkins, Dionne Griffiths, Julie Stacey, Ros Huntley and Janet Sandhu. Thank you, all, your input has been invaluable. A mention also to Thomas Padley, thanks for giving me some guitar knowledge.

Special thanks as ever go out to Angela, Jodie and Melissa for allowing me the time to write.

Note to the reader:

In this story songs play an important role: an aspect that will become clear when you read on. I would like to encourage you to listen to the songs that are mentioned when they appear at certain points in the narrative. They can all be found by searching Youtube. I believe listening to them will enhance the journey you take with the principle character. If you'd prefer not to do so, I have hopefully written in such a way that the atmosphere bleeds from the text regardless.

These words now belong to you; I hope you enjoy them.

CHAPTER

1

The sense of being in the wrong place, with absolutely no idea where the right place might be, is an unnerving feeling that destroys any chance of rational thought. Amid this confusion, my body refuses to hold onto the gasps of air that my lungs are desperately crying out for. My head swims through a lack of oxygen, and even as the suffocating voice in my head says *calm down, breathe deeper, breathe more slowly,* panic continues to rule for at least five minutes.

Eventually, feeling like a man who came close to drowning before being cast upon a foreign shore, I do manage to calm somewhat. I've literally just woken from sleep, and I'm sitting in the driver's seat of a car. It's freezing, and I fumble the keys from where they sit on the central console into the ignition. Start the engine. Turn the heat up to max and ramp the fan to full blast.

A coating of frost on the inside of the windscreen has not yet begun to clear, and the cold air blowing through the vents sends a shudder through my bones as it stirs the resident aroma of night-breath and flatulence. I realise at that moment the bigger question is not, *where am I?* It's, *who am I?* Eventually the heat from the ticking engine kicks in and begins to lick the bottom of the ice-coated screen.

It's punishingly cold. As yet, the engine's heat is barely penetrating my skin, but I don't believe any rise in temperature would remove the chill of fear that kicks my heart into a fresh flutter of renewed anxiety.

Why would I sleep in a car when it's so cold? To the silent question I have no answer. Perhaps not the most salient question I could have asked myself, but it is what comes to my mind as I desperately try to remain calm. *Wearing…?* A quick glance down reveals a suit. The material is dark, somewhat crumpled – no surprise, being as I've slept in it – and hardly suitable for such conditions.

Whoever I am, it would appear I'm the kind of person who owns and wears a suit. A quick exploration of the pockets reveals nothing other than a thick wad of twenties that are held together with a large clip. I have nothing else on me. Nothing up my sleeve, nothing in my pockets, and nothing in my damn head that gives even the slightest clue to who I might be.

The frost on the outside of the glass has reacted to the heat of the blower, and is now crazed with half-melt shapes that the wipers clear with ease. Dribbles of moisture follow the returning blade and trickle down the glass, distorting a view that's fogged with a haze of condensation on the inside. *As tears go by*, I think, and a mournful tune strums in my mind. Other words accompany the imagined music. The words may or may not be lyrics to an actual song. They come with an easy rhythm, so I guess they probably are genuine lyrics. *As tears go by*. That's just what they look like, and they reflect my emotion. I feel like crying for real but hold the flood back with a tremulous breath that shudders down the aching length of my spine.

The car is parked on a hill. Not quite the top, I realise, glancing over my shoulder to look out of the rear window, through wide bands that have cleared much more quickly than the front. On the rear seat is a leather coat. I drag it into the front, my attention snared by an elderly guy sauntering down the opposite pavement with a Yorkshire terrier in tow. Forgetting the guy for the moment I check the pockets of the coat. The fragrance of the leather is comforting, but it wouldn't really sit well with the suit, and I wonder if it actually belongs to me. Putting the jacket on the passenger seat, I look out to see the guy and his dog have diverted along a side street named Sycamore Avenue, where rows of naked trees overhang a string of parked cars, their crystalline white roofs sparkling and silent. Before me, through glass still partially obscured with mist, I see that the road drops steeply and disappears around a bend. The hill bottoms out to a wide flat vista that stretches towards an ice-fogged horizon. A motorway flyover with two decks carries early morning traffic past a large shopping mall, a mall that stands on a steelwork's grave.

Steelworks?

A memory?

Possibly.

Invented?

Maybe.

Is it a conjured figment? Is it the invention of a mind that's desperately clutching for a grasp of reality? Invention is a high likelihood, because the clumsy grasp of thought attracts nothing else.

I'm reminded of those cranes in arcades on the coast.

If only I could remember something meaningful, something personal. "ANYTHING!" I yell, bashing my fist against the side window. The old guy jumps back a step and glares at me for a moment before pulling his dog into a yapping tumble. From twenty paces into the side street he pauses to look back and glares some more. A distinct air of tension fills the void between us.

Maybe he's trying to memorise the registration number of the car. *Good,* I try to transmit. *If you find out who I am, come back and let me know.*

Unless it's not my car. With that thought my mind and my eyes switch to the glove compartment. Maybe that will house a clue: paperwork, registration documents, a name. The car's interior is now toasty warm. My fingers feel numb from the temperature transition as they curl with some unexplainable trepidation into the catch. The compartment door flops open to reveal a book, a journal. It's quite large, the size of a large envelope. *A4,* I think, *or is it A3?* Whichever, the journal is lilac in colour and over an inch thick, weighty, with a cover that's deeply embossed with a repeated flower symbol. Judging by the crumpled dark-grey suit and plain black shoes, I'm guessing it's not mine. The journal is held shut by a wide strip of elastic, also lilac and attached to the back cover by silver rivets. Trapped under the elastic is a slip of white paper. There's a message written on it in rather elegant writing – big and loopy and most definitely feminine. *Tom, please read this,* the inky-blue swirls entreat.

Tom?

Am I Tom? As the 'T' flicks my tongue to the roof of my mouth, as my lips softly close and then part around the 'm', the clumsy claws of my mind slip over the sound it makes. The name means nothing. I try, desperately, to make it mean something – try to push levers that offer no control. *Hi, I'm Tom…* There's no flood of memory accompanying the name. Absolutely nothing.

The use of the word *please* suggests that whoever wrote on the slip of paper is not entirely convinced that Tom will read it, be that me or someone else. To my mind, right now, the word suggests a measure of desperation.

Loosely gripping the journal, tapping the cover with my thumb, I lean over the passenger seat and, while inhaling the fragrance of leather, look into the depth of the glove compartment. A pen. Nothing else. It glints with a metallic purple sheen. Whoever placed the journal in there likely placed the pen in there too, likely placed it in there after writing the note of pleading and slipping it under the elastic strap.

Please read this.

Please…

An overwhelming sense of foreboding surges into my mind and I swallow dryly as I stretch the binding-elastic aside and prepare to open the cover.

CHAPTER

2

An envelope has been inserted between the cover and the first page. Pink in colour, it is the kind that would likely be purchased with a birthday card. Embossed on the flap is the logo of the manufacturer. On the verge of breaking into the sealed envelope, the nail of the thumb on my right hand distracts me. The nail is long for a man and manicured to the point of femininity, as are the nails on my fingers. *Maybe the lilac journal is mine after all. Perhaps the pink envelope is for me too.* This thought is partially erased when I notice all of the nails on my left hand have been bitten to extreme shortness. A small personal detail, it shows complete polarity but offers no explanation that I can think of.

The yap of a small dog pulls me from contemplating this unusual discovery any further and I look up to see the same guy that passed by earlier. He's heading back in my direction, along the side street with a certain manner in his walk that looks somewhat like fear cloaked in bravery. His shoulders are elevated, his chest puffed, elbows out to the side, but his pace is slow and hesitant. A cloud of icy-breath partially masks his face. The dog's lead is taut with canine eagerness. When he's almost level with me, only the road's width separating us, I open the window. The whine of the motor seems incredibly loud, the window opens with impossible slowness, and I imagine him taking off before I have a chance to speak. No doubt hearing the window, he halts with a flinch, glances my way, and there he stands – his little dog yip-yip-yapping – hovering between maintaining his bravado and scampering back down Sycamore Avenue to his rear.

"Sorry about before… banging the window."

He rolls his lower jaw, and yanks the lead as the dog yaps with an extra measure of vigour. "S'alright," he finally says, his accent thick with Northern brusqueness, the blend of words more of a sound, a grunt; it's a masculine-nod to the fact that we can move on without the need for further niceties.

"Can you tell me–?"

"SHURRUP!" he snaps, cutting short my question, giving the dog's leash a firm tug that makes very little impression on its constant yap.

I wait while he glares at the still-yapping dog a moment, before trying again when he looks up at me. "Can you please tell me where I am?"

He frowns a little and looks around, almost as if

unsure himself. "Wincobank, mate."

Again, empty claws grasp at a meaningless word. As if it's been engineered that way, no prize is forthcoming from this arcade-crane. The name means nothing to me.

"Where is, Wincobank?"

The frown folds into the deeper creases of a scowl. "Yer takin' the piss?"

No need for words, I shake my head. Sorrow or some other expression that elicits empathy must show on my face, for his scowl softens.

"Lost are yer?"

"Yep," I state, trying my utmost to sound chummy while swallowing the bubbling sensation of upset that tries to steal into my voice as I take a quick glance towards the motorway beyond the skirt of the hill.

"Yer in Sheffield. Gerroff the motorway too early, did yer?"

Sheffield I've heard of. Birthplace of steel, I think. Maybe that earlier recollection of steelworks was a memory. "Yeh, something like that." With a nod of thanks, I close the window, shutting out the biting cold, and watch through the side mirror as he makes his way back up the hill.

Turning my attention to the envelope, keen to open it, I discover that curiosity works in mysterious ways. Curiosity stops me from opening it straight away and forces me to first see if a name has been written on the flipside. There is no name, but there is a mass of hastily scribbled text. Despite the rushed appearance, it looks to be in the same hand as the looped writing that was trapped under the elastic.

I only just thought to put this in here at the last minute, when I realised what day tomorrow was. Thought these pictures might help. Hope so. Sorry! I know that might not make any sense. Hope you're OK? Hope we're OK? Please read the book.
Love Penny X

My hands are shaking as I break the seal and lift the envelope's flap. I'm somewhat fearful. The dread of it not being meant for me, I guess. *Penny?* The name means as little to me as Tom, but I hope that Penny is someone I know. Three uses of *hope* in such a short message screams of concern. If it is meant for me, that concern is surely justified.

From the envelope I draw a photograph. It's a picture of a woman who looks to be in her early-twenties. She's sitting on a wall and behind her is a sea that glistens with an aqua hue. She has vibrant blue eyes and dark copper hair that runs down to and frames a cleavage my eye struggles to pull away from. A few strands of her hair appear to be caught on a breeze: gentle, I'm guessing, and warm, if the thin-strapped summer dress is anything to go by. On the reverse is written: *Penny – Lanzarote, 2012.*

Sadly, the picture of her has not resurrected a memory. If I were not so panicked it may have implanted desire; it has raised my curiosity, but it hasn't aroused a memory. I reach inside the envelope again, hoping more than ever that Penny is someone I know.

Another photo stares back at me. This one holds a picture of a man. At a guess, he looks a couple of years older than Penny. He has sandy coloured hair that is almost down to his shoulders, and dark eyes. In this picture they're too dark to truly identify the colour. He's standing thigh deep in a wide hole in the ground, leaning against a spade. My mind instantly turns to a sinister reason and decides it's a grave. He's smiling though, so I guess it's not. He's bare-chested, sun-kissed, and toned with muscles that look to have been earned through hard graft, from work done outside of a gym. On the reverse, in the same big loopy writing, someone, presumably Penny, has written: *Tom, digging pond for Kaitlyn's mum.*

Tom looks a good match for Penny, and I figuratively cross every finger and toe as I tilt the rear-view mirror in my direction.

CHAPTER

3

Discovering that the pond-digging Tom looks the same as the face in the mirror, my bleak void is filled with a swirl of elated illumination. The feeling is immediately washed away with an overwhelming flood of wretched disappointment.

Why do I not recall digging a pond?

Why do the names mean nothing to me?

Who is Penny?

Who is Kaitlyn?

Maybe I just look like this person, this ditch-digging Tom. A quick check of my biceps and pectoral muscles indicates that I have not only his appearance but also his physique. I'd hoped for blue eyes. Don't know why. Maybe it's because Penny's look so much nicer than the slightly greenish-brown eyes looking back at me.

Why do I have no memory of the intriguing Penny-in-Lanzarote? Sorry, Penny, but your pictures haven't worked. Your three hopes have proven to be as useful as my recent wishes.

In the time it's taken to warm up the car's interior, to scare the wits out of an old guy and his yapping dog, to discover I'm situated on a hill in a place called Wincobank in the City of Sheffield, to find out I'm Tom-who-once-dug-a-pond who has a connection, hopefully, to a captivating girl named Penny, the sky has greyed over. The light rain that's accompanied this greyness has washed away the frost with its freeze of sparkling promise and replaced it with a dreary despair that patters on top of the car's roof.

Please read this, the slip of paper requested. *Please read this,* meaning the journal. Putting the pictures back in the envelope, placing them on top of the leather coat on the passenger seat beside the note of pleading, I prepare to do just that.

* * *

26ᵗʰ January 2015

If you're reading this...

This is weird. I don't know whether to use you or I...

OK. If you are reading this, and don't know why, if you've no recollection of writing it, then you're a fucking weirdo who not only can't remember anything that happened for the first twenty years of his life, but apparently also disappears every year for just over a week, and can't remember doing that either.

OK. I'm going to start again. Penelope has just looked over my shoulder and she's not happy. Says I've got to take this seriously or we're over. Now. Finito! I don't want us to be over, how about you, Tom? May I call you Tom?

Here goes. My name is Tom Gardener. The "Gardener" bit is invented, because I don't know what my surname is. I might have invented the Tom bit too, but I don't think so. Don't know why, it just sort of fits.

Yesterday morning, Penny woke me up and she was pretty pissed with me. Well, with you actually, because maybe you're the one that remembers. Do you?

Going off track, sorry. I never claimed to be a writer...

Penny woke me up, almost tipped me off the sofa. She asked where I'd been, again!!! Actually she screeched the "again". I didn't have a clue what she was on about. I couldn't, and still can't, remember a thing. But I do have the God of all headaches. I had assumed

I'd gone out and got pissed, that I'd fallen asleep downstairs, and couldn't remember going out. She claims I've been missing for eight days. Says I did the same last year, but for seven days. Says I've done the same thing every January since moving in with her, three years back in November 2012.

She reckons it might have something to do with me not being able to remember anything before the age of twenty (that age is also a guess, by the way, which would make me 28 right now, and you 29, if you're reading this a year from now). That is something I actually do remember, the not being able to remember anything before the guessed at age of twenty. It's only last May when we had an argument that I told Penny about it.

I'm sure this is all a bit confusing, but it should make sense eventually.

Anyway, Pen came up with this idea of me keeping a journal. Not a journal, exactly, she said journal, but I reckon that'd just be like a diary. I'm meant to write about stuff that's happened in the past, not just stuff that happened on the day I'm writing. Her idea is that if you - weird again - I read it then some sort of mixed-up memory puzzle might all slot into place. So this is meant to... invoke *memories, I suppose.*

I think she's thinking some kind of yin-yang scenario. That during this missing week, I/you might remember the time before I was 20, but not know about the life I've lived for the other 51 weeks of the year ever since. That kind of worries me though, the yin-yang thing. I can't help thinking good and bad, because my life with Penelope is really good. And, well, you get the picture.

* * *

Can what I've just read in this journal be true? I've only read the first couple of pages, and it's pretty heavy stuff. I guess I do get the picture: he's… I'm worried that something might be unearthed that will ultimately ruin things. My mind burns with the enormity of what I've just read. I'm sorry, Tom, I haven't a clue about the first twenty years of your life. I have nothing, good, bad, or otherwise.

Am I to believe that I wrote this? Or is it some kind of a cruel joke, a psychological experiment? I suppose it's all I have. For now, I'm prepared to accept it.

I'm aching to read more, to see if anything stirs in my mind, but I can't. Not yet. My head is pounding.

God of all headaches! It's not a phrase that those slippery claws of memory are readily grasping. My gut is crying out for food, though, and right now it's shouting slightly louder than my anxiety. I've no idea what the date is, and no idea when I last ate, so I determine to rectify both of these situations in the Mall at the bottom of the hill before reading any further.

CHAPTER

4

I hope Tom is looking at the picture this frame normally holds. With tears in my eyes and concern on my mind, I hold the empty frame to my chest. Ironically, I hope he's looking at the picture of me and doesn't have a clue about who I am. He didn't come home last night, as expected. But, if the past three Januaries are anything to go by, he'll return in seven to nine days. If those past years are any indication, he will claim not to know where he's been, claim not to know, and even be shocked that he's been missing for a week. If the pictures don't work, if the journal doesn't work, when he returns, he'll get all upset as I manage to convince him that not only is it true, it's happened before.

Not for the first time, I ask myself if I believe him. Do I genuinely believe that he disappears for just over a week, only to return and not remember a thing about it? As a couple, we're great together; always have been since the day we met. As of the May before last, I now have to include, *do I believe that he can't remember anything of his life before the age of twenty?* I have to believe him, for now. If I don't, it means everything we have is wrapped around a lie.

It strikes me as ironic that Tom can't remember most of his past, while I wish I could forget a chunk of mine.

Hearing footfalls on the landing, I quickly place the frame on the sideboard. My finger catches the back as I hastily withdraw my hand, and it clatters face down.

"You OK, Pen?"

I didn't want questions. Perhaps I shouldn't have looked at the frame while Kaitlyn popped to the loo. "I'm fine." Leaving the frame face down, I look up at my friend, leaning over the banister.

"You don't look fine. Look like you're on the verge of crying."

I make my way to the kitchen, putting some distance between the toppled-frame and me as Kaitlyn skips down the remaining steps.

"You've been a bit distant all week." Kaitlyn stretches the end of the sentence and I turn in the kitchen doorway to see that she's picked up the frame and is looking at me with investigative eyes.

"What's going on, Pen? Is Tom really away on business? Is he fucking someone – the shit – is that it? Is that why…?" She holds up the frame that only yesterday held a picture of Tom digging the hole for a pond in her mum's garden. She's no doubt imagining it ripped up in the bin. Her eye then drifts to the wall and settles on the empty frame that previously held a picture of me in Lanzarote, a picture that Kaitlyn took when we holidayed there together. She's aware that it's Tom's favourite picture of me. More than once he's thanked her for her photographic skills. Pure chance, in reality, but his comment never failed to bring a smile to her face.

"No," I manage, shaking my head, trying to erase the image that Kaitlyn has implanted. "It's missing because…" Blubbering tears wash aside further words of explanation, the reason for why the picture frames are empty, for why Tom is absent. It's an explanation I had no intention of voicing.

* * *

Kaitlyn firms her lower jaw, gazes at me a while longer, then downs the remainder of her now tepid coffee. "He can't remember? I'm not sure if that's the worst or best excuse I've ever heard, but I don't believe it. You know what – if it's an annual thing – I bet he's got a kid, somewhere. I mean, how could someone disappear for a week and not remember? It'll be the kid's birthday, something like that… Or, maybe he's having an affair and she keeps quiet on the understanding that she gets a full week with him once a year. Or…"

Credit where it's due, Kaitlyn not only listened while I explained the situation, she shushes the instant I hold up my hand. "You're not saying anything I've not already thought of, Kait. One time, I even Googled *calendar events in January,* to see if that gave light to anything. Apparently in January it's *World Braille Day.* I convinced myself he was having an affair with a deaf woman, going to conventions with her. I practised some sign language and tried a few phrases on him. He looked at me like I was crazy, gave me some signs of his own when I accused him of shagging a deaf woman. So, come up with any scenario you can think of, Kait. I doubt you'll beat that one."

Kaitlyn smirks, which irritates me, and then really annoys me when it stretches into a grin.

"What?"

"You do know braille is for blind people?" Kaitlyn nods her head.

"Oh!" The realisation, and the eye-rolling look on my friend's face instantly dissolve my building irritation. "I do know that. Of course I know that. Can't think why my brain automatically went down the road of deaf person."

"Signing is more dramatic than reading bumps on paper, I suppose. I don't think that would have had quite the same amount of drama." Kaitlyn sniffs, suddenly turning semi-serious. "I'm going to need another coffee before we carry on talking about this. I could do with a spot of lunch too, my–"

"I don't want to talk about it."

"Then why'd you ask me to come over?"

Kaitlyn emulates the shrug of my shoulders. "Just wanted some company, s'pose. Take my mind off it."

While shaking her head, Kaitlyn forms a sympathetic expression. "You actually really do believe him, don't you? You really believe he goes away on the same day in January, every year, comes back a week or so later, and that he can't remember a thing? We need to talk about this Pen, and we're going to."

"Not now," I say with a self-pitying sigh. "Maybe tomorrow."

C H A P T E R

5

27th January 2015

Hello my future self. Sorry about the ripped out page. What you're reading here is my second attempt at January 27th. Penny objected to the explicit details I wrote about last night, and insisted I start over. If she gets bored of looking, I'll fill you in later ;~)

She's accusing me of not taking this seriously, now. Again.

Penny thinks the best place to start this is at the beginning of what I do remember, but if the point of this is to stir up memories, I think it'd be best to write about Penny. She plays the central role in all my fondest memories, which is where this post originally began. We made a great memory last night (censored version). Can't beat making up for something you don't remember, and if you can't recall what happened, wow, we really have got no hope.

Before I go on, I've just written our landline and address on the inside back cover. For now, here, I'll just say that you live in Surrey. I imagine you (still feels weird, but I can't quite manage to refer to myself in the future in this context as I). I imagine I'd want to phone Penny right away and say come and get me. Or I'd feel like getting in a taxi and saying, take me to this address. I hope you don't. I want to get to the bottom of this, I think (scared of finding out something bad, like I'm... I don't know, like I'm some kind of bad guy, or something). So, anyway, I'm hoping you'll continue reading this. I'm hoping you'll stay wherever you are and find stuff out. It might be a good idea to write in a book too. Write down anything you remember while you're there, wherever there is. Anything might help.

OK, here goes.

I first met Penelope Wilkes in 2010 on September the 10th. She was celebrating her twenty-first birthday. The earliest memory I have - which I'll get to later - is three years and eight months before that date. Over that time I made a living from cash in hand jobs, gardening at first, then playing a guitar and singing in bars. I guess I learned to play the guitar at some point in my forgotten past, and I'm better at it than I am at gardening. I was playing a gig in a pub called the Pig and Whistle when Penny caught my eye. The pub was packed, but I sang to her alone, all night, hoping she wouldn't leave before I'd had a chance to speak to her. Never took my eyes away from hers. Except when she went to the loo of course, that would have freaked her out. When she leaned over the bar to order a drink my eyes were fixed. Man, those dark jeans did her justice.

I went to chat to her when I took a break. She thought I'd been singing to her mate, Kaitlyn. Kait is good looking, and she's a lovely person, but something about Penny just captured me. I can't really say why. I'll just say she looks interesting, intriguing. Her nose scrunches when she smiles. I love that. Anyway, she blushed like a beetroot when I said I'd been singing to her. That captivated me even more.

Turns out the two of them were at Uni together, training to be nurses. I bought Penny a drink for her birthday and asked if she wanted to request a song. Couldn't believe it when she requested Bieber's "Baby". Our relationship was nearly over there and then, before it had even began. All night I'd been covering classic rock tracks (couldn't stand most of the popular late nineties music, and 2010 didn't offer anything much better). I'm singing rock and she wanted Bieber. Months later, she confessed that she'd been winding me up. If you were here now you'd see me laughing. Weird again. You are me. Duh! Anyway, back then, when I thought she was being serious, after telling her I didn't know the words, I made amends by singing another song with baby in the lyrics, a much better one: Aerosmith's "Angel". It's now her favourite song, but it could easily have been one she hated. I really hammed it up, pointing to her as I sang about being in love, indicating that she was the one that my tears were for. In some way, despite only just meeting her, I meant it. The way Penny used both hands to cover her embarrassment was delightful. She peered at me through her fingers while Kaitlyn chuckled in the chair next to her.

Back then, those lyrics meant more to me than she could possibly have known. As I sang,

I truly meant almost every line. I guess it was a cry for help as much as anything. But I don't need to tell you that. The closing lyrics will mean more to you as you read this than they mean to me as I write.

* * *

Looking away from the pages, tears are stinging behind my eyes as what are surely lyrics to the Aerosmith song stream into my mind: the singer pleading for his baby, his angel, to come and save him tonight. I close the journal, because I can't focus on the words anyway. Sniffing away tears that finally manage to break free, wiping them with my sleeve, I glance around the food hall full of hungry shoppers and catch the eye of a middle-aged woman who's sitting alone. She throws me a smile of sympathy before tipping her eyes back into a novel. As the mentioned Aerosmith song illustrates, I really am alone, but I genuinely don't know if I can face the rest of the day, let alone the night. I'm only just managing to resist turning to the back cover, only just managing to resist phoning the number that I've supposedly written there. I could go home now to a woman who's supposedly my angel, but I'd be going home without answers. I need… I want answers, but like the writing in this lilac journal indicates, I'm also afraid of what I might discover.

The long nails on only one hand now make sense at least. As do the graft-earned muscles. Neither of these things feel like memory though and, as pleasing as it is to have the knowledge, I may as well be reading a novel, like the woman over there.

The heady mix of fried onions, charred meat, and herby-garlic pizza is making me feel a little nauseous, and the gurgle of drink fizzing around the greasy chicken in my gut is in danger of making a reappearance if I stay much longer. I decide to take my own advice and buy a small notebook – don't think I'm going to have much to write down though – and then set out in search of some cheap room for the night. I'm also going to buy an Aerosmith CD, see if listening to 'Angel' is more successful in bringing an image of Penny to my mind than this writing has been. I need to feel Penny in my heart. I need to see her smile and scrunched nose in my mind. The photograph of Penny is like the cover on a novel, and the writing has given me an essence, but she still feels nothing more than fictional.

What does that make me?

Until my memories return, I will never feel real. Until my memories return, I really am just a character in an unfinished book.

C H A P T E R

6

Set back from any major roads, nestled in amongst woodland, the expansive garden is cast dark and blue, and is lit only by the slenderest crescent of moonlight. An owl hoots in the distance, softly pushing against the silence before taking flight on a whisper of feather. The night is cold, but the temperature has not plummeted to the frigid depths that January nights are capable of reaching. The garden shed is unlocked and will provide decent shelter. Despite the shroud of darkness, it is not late. At seven-thirty in the evening, many people will not yet be home from work. A quick glance at the large house, nestled in the centre of its large grounds, shows what looks to be lamplight in an upstairs window. Presumably the owner is retiring early, for there is no light in any of the ground-floor rooms.

He hears footsteps on the narrow track road and peers through a gap in the fence. The advancing steps are coming down the slope, heading towards the canal and the houses beyond. It's more than likely just someone taking a shortcut through the narrow band of woods. The person is not yet in view, but he guesses the footfalls are female from the snapping sound of a sharp-heel striking tarmac. A woman. Alone, unless her company is wearing shoes that fall as softly as the owl's feathers took flight.

He waits, standing still, keeping quiet. The owl hoots in the distance and another replies. There she is. She stops and listens, then glances around in every direction other than the fence. She looks into the trees at the other side of the track, her posture tense. Maybe she heard him moving from the front of the shed and making his way through the overgrown shrubbery. No doubt she considers the fence a strong barrier, as something that need not be feared. Fear, concern, is reserved for the open trees and darkness on the other side of the track.

Without seeing her face it's hard to tell, but through the knothole in the fence she looks young. She has a nice figure. Boots with high heels, silver buckles on the side. She has long hair that coils and waves down to the middle of her back. Feeling as lonely as he does, she is as welcome a sight as he could have hoped for.

She moves on, continues down the track, heading towards the canal. It's maybe ten or twelve minutes walk at that pace. She would then only have to cross the bridge and she'd be walking along the well-lit streets across from the train station. At this time the main road will be busy with commuters. Not here though, not on this track, not on a dark and cold January evening. Even at seven-thirty, at this time of year, a place like this is practically deserted, the very reason he chose this spot.

He clambers over the fence quickly, not too concerned at this stage if he makes a sound. But surprise might just give him an advantage, so he carefully lowers himself rather than jump. A compromise reached between speed and silence he rushes the few paces she has advanced during the time it took him to make a decision.

As she's pushed to the ground, face down, cheek pressed into the cold tarmac, a knee pressing between her shoulder blades, she doesn't even scream. She makes sounds of protest, but it's more of a pitiful whimper, a barely decipherable 'no, please, no'. She tries to prevent her belt from being unfastened, until she receives a heavy fist, a crunching blow to the side of her head. She breaks into racking sobs, as she lets go of the belt and covers her head against the possibility of another thump. Suddenly, it's about survival and nothing else.

Her belt undone, the jeans and knickers are soon down to her knees, her hips scraping and banging the tarmac as she's entered with harsh inconsideration.

* * *

I wake with a panic-filled gasp and realise it was just a dream. A nightmare. *Maybe it's all been a dream*, I dare to hope, as I take in surroundings that are lit by spears of streetlight, the vertical blinds that stink of collected dust drawing dark stripes through a yellow cast on the wall opposite.

There is nothing amiss with my short-term memory.

The damp, musky dog-like smell of the cheap

room confirms the fact. Glad that I paid for only one night, I try to breathe shallowly against the background aroma of semen. I could easily call the fifteen-quid a loss and hire somewhere else, somewhere a little more expensive, somewhere that doesn't have a shared toilet decorated with an amber crust and stray pubic hairs. I could do that, simply leave, but I have no way of knowing how far the wad of twenties needs to stretch.

I can't believe that dream; it felt so real.

Reaching for the lilac journal that's slid to the floor, switching on the lamp, I wonder if maybe it's a memory, a memory that came to me unbidden when I nodded off.

Am I a rapist?

No… it was just a dream, a nightmare. My worst fears slipping into my mind when I'm at my most vulnerable. Surely Penny would know. Surely she wouldn't be with someone like that. I think back to the disclosure of a missing twenty years, a disclosure that I have supposedly written. The dread of possibility rises through the fog of my mind. It was just a bad dream, surely, a bad dream that was inspired by the earlier sound of someone banging a prostitute in the next room. I should have spent a little more money. Even another tenner would have garnered a room in a better place than this.

I can't read any more about Penny, not in this

room, not with that horrid dream fresh in my mind. From what I've read so far, she sounds amazing. If I'm to believe the words I've supposedly written, I love her loads. I wish she felt as real as the dream. Not for the first time, I'm sorely tempted to look in the back cover for the telephone number, but I'm not going to. I'm not going back to Penny, not until she feels real, not until I feel whole.

The door in the next room creaks open and then slams shut. A few minutes of silence follows. No soft owl hoots in here. Low voices in the room, muffled, but clearly one male and one female. Movement. The sound of a bed's springs creaking. Then the bed bangs against the wall, its rhythm increasing in both speed and volume. Five minutes pass before a male voice grunts an expulsion of pleasure.

That's it; I've had enough.

Fuck the fifteen-quid.

There's no way I'm going to sleep in that bed anyway. If I run out of money before this is over, tough.

I'd rather freeze to death in the car than spend another minute in here.

CHAPTER

7

No point freezing in the car until I've actually run out of money, but based on the amount of time the book indicates I'm going to be here, I figured I couldn't afford a room at a decent budget hotel. So, finding The Foundry was a blessing. It's a smallish boozer. The room's pretty basic, but it's clean, and there's breakfast thrown in for £26 a night.

The beer's not bad, and other than a couple of lads playing pool, the place is quiet.

I've read plenty in this journal about how much I love Penny. Penelope. Pen. No form of the name strikes a chord, but I'm inclined to believe it; I just wish I felt it. I'm curious to know what happened when I arrived in Surrey. If I knew nothing of the time before I arrived, I guess, not knowing how I got there and not knowing who I was, would have felt like I do right now. Rather strange that I'm empathising with my younger self as if it were a different person. Somehow, it seems I coped, and I didn't have a journal to explain it all. The fact that I managed back then, is somewhat calming.

The lilac journal stares at me from the table. The black notebook sits beside it with the metallic purple pen on top. I've not written anything in it yet. I've nothing worth writing about. Except…

Opening the notebook, I take a moment to order the words in my mind, tapping a rhythm between my lower lip and upper teeth with the pen that surely belongs to Penny.

16th January 2016: Woke up in car, parked on a hill at a place called Wincobank in the City of Sheffield. Don't know who I am, other than what I've read in this book. Can't remember anything. No memories at all, except steelworks, possibly. Maybe I've been here before. Found a room in a pub called The Foundry.

As much as I've enjoyed reading about Penny, I put the notebook down and pick up the journal hoping that it moves on to something new, hoping that I'm writing about something else. I note from the opening paragraphs of the new entry that, despite being rather depressed, I have.

"Anything interesting?"

I immediately close the journal and look up.

The barmaid hovers over me with a couple of empty, froth-coated glasses in her hand. She's cute, petite, with a chiselled face. Pixie-like. Her hair is choppy and quite short, and dyed a brilliant shade of red. She's wearing a lacy dark blue dress with tatty red sneakers. It's a combination that really shouldn't work, but it kind of does. I pull my eyes away from her, and notice the lads that were playing pool have left.

"Not sure yet." It's all I'm prepared to give. I'm not about to say, *I wrote it, but I don't remember doing so.*

"Room OK?"

"Fine, thanks."

She hovers a moment, her hips swinging slightly, her eye flicking to the notebook and the pen sitting next to the almost empty pint pot I've been drinking from. I back the words up with a small smile, and raise my eyebrows as if to say, *anything else?*

"Get you another?" Tipping her head, she indicates the finger's width of ale. "On the house, being as you're a guest and there's only us in here."

There's a naughty sounding edge to the inflection she places on *only us*.

"Always this quiet?" I ask, before drinking the last drop and handing her the glass. "Thanks." It's a little late coming but, in fairness, I am a little distracted.

"Mid-week, it is."

As she walks away, I can't help but admire her figure. There's no ring on her left hand, I notice, and I think of my empty room on the first floor. An image of Penny floods my mind and fills me with guilt. *If it weren't for the journal and the photographs I would not have been aware of Penny. In that light, would I have tried to get the barmaid up there? Asked, not forced,* I quickly push into my mind. *Have I done so before?* I can't remember yesterday, never mind this exact same date last year.

"Except if we have a function," she continues from behind the bar, as she pulls on the pump lever, an attractive look of concentration fixed on the glass. "Landlord reckons it used to be packed every night before they shut down the steelworks. Before my time though; I were only a little-un when they built Meadowhall."

"Was it steel works then? Where the shopping mall is?"

"Shopping mall? What are you, American?" She chuckles at that, quietly repeating *shopping mall* to herself with an American twang. "Yeh, steelworks. A lot of the land around it was, too."

A shiver traces my spine, and my skin tingles as if a hundred spiders have skittered across my flesh. In my mind I hear the steady rhythmic thump of a large hammer.

"You OK?" she asks, as I take the glass from her and knock back a big swallow of its contents. "You look a bit pale." Foam clings to the glass in much the same way as the sound of that hammer clings to my thoughts.

"Just getting over a cold," I lie.

She nods her understanding. "You're not from around here?"

Wish I could be as certain as you. The words almost slip from my tongue, and I realise it's a question, not a statement.

"Only, you not knowing about the steelworks. You up here to do with work?"

Perhaps I should have stayed in the room. "Looking into my past." *Near enough the truth.*

"Like family history, you mean?"

With a straight-lipped smile, I give a nod of affirmation. I don't want to be rude. She's pleasant company. It's just I'm desperate to read more of this journal. It's got to the part when I first landed down south at the approximate age of twenty: my earliest memory, apparently. I notice her eyes tipping to the journal in my lap.

"Me mum does that. She uses the library for it. It's free there, you know, *finding your past*. If you wanted to use it... They your notes?"

A hint of smirk comes to her lips as she widens her eyes. The twist of her mouth indicates that she's trying to prevent it from curving into a broad grin. I can't help but smile myself as I give the cover a tap.

"Those are my notes." I indicate the small black notebook sitting on the table. "Not much in there yet. I'm hoping the stuff in this book will be helpful though."

"Right," she says, half turning away, looking over her shoulder and giving me a cheeky wink. "Thought it looked a bit girly. I'll leave you to it then…"

She allows the sentence to fade into an expectant look, as if she's asked a question and is waiting for the answer.

"Tom," I say with an air of confidence, assuming she was waiting for my name. That's something I couldn't have done first thing this morning. "My name is Tom."

"Nicky."

"Right, thanks. Thanks for the drink, Nicky."

Just then, an old chap enters the pub, dragging the cold night air behind him. He walks across the room with purpose, his slight limp assisted by a stick that has a bulbous end rather than a hook. Tucking the stick under his arm, he briskly rubs his hands before removing a flat cap from his head. I notice Nicky is already pulling him a pint as he heads for the bar, tucking the folded cap into his coat pocket.

"By heck; it's wicked cold out, lass," he says.

"Like me to make you a cup of tea instead?" Nicky chuckles and throws me a broad smile.

"Tea? Don't be daft. I've me missus at home if I want tea."

The old guy fishes a wallet from his trouser pocket. It's fat with notes that he tucks back into place as he pulls out a tenner. "Take one for yersen," he says, ramming the wallet home as he swaps the note for the pint.

"Thanks Arthur." Nicky throws me a smile. "I'll have one later, if that's alright?"

"As yer like lass," he says, before knocking back half of the pint and wiping the froth from his upper lip with the back of his hand.

A regular, I realise, and let their continuing conversation become background noise as I open the journal and glance at the door. *Wicked cold…* I'll say it is. And I hate it. I hate the cold. I hate the darkness of night too, preferring instead the long days of summer. *Is that the way I've always felt?* I wonder. *Or, is it a preference I've only just established.*

Maybe the Journal has the answer.

CHAPTER

8

1ˢᵗ February 2015

Felt really down for the last couple of days, and couldn't be bothered with writing this.

Sorry, I know that's no help to you.

This missing week business, has hit me harder than the void of the missing twenty years before I built this life I have with Penny. I think I'm scared that I might wake up one day and have to start over yet again, that I'll have forgotten my time in Surrey with this wonderful woman.

I don't want that to happen, so there's more reason than ever to continue with this.

I've already written that the first twenty years of my life is a mystery. Roughly twenty. Can't be certain. I might've been an old looking eighteen year old. I might've been a young looking twenty-four. Don't know why I decided I was twenty. Like the name, Tom, it just felt right.

Here's how it began. One day, the first day my memory stretches back to, I woke up in a shop doorway. Freezing. Surprised I didn't die. Turns out I was in London. I had money in my pocket: £240, in twenties. I hadn't a clue who I was, or where I'd come from. No idea where I'd got the money from either. Maybe I'd nicked it. Maybe I'd mugged someone. I haven't a clue. First thing I did was head for a café I spotted on the other side of the road. I wolfed down a sausage and tomato bap as if I'd not eaten for a week. Burnt my mouth. Got a right glare from the woman when I took a swig of coffee and quickly spat it onto the floor. Discovered I don't like coffee, anyway.

From a newspaper in the café I discovered it was 2007, January 22nd. I recall realising how much I detested that cold and dark month. Maybe I always have. I still hate those nights when it gets dark early, especially if it's really cold.

After warming in the café, two mugs of tea later, I exited onto busy bustling streets. After spending so much time getting warm in the café, it felt even colder outdoors. I needed somewhere to think, somewhere warm, somewhere to get my head around things, to decide what I was going to do.

I headed for the tube station along the road.

I missed a train by seconds, but what did that matter. I was in no rush to get anywhere. On the empty platform, I took a bench seat and waited, leaning forward, forearms resting on my thighs looking towards the empty black mouth that would eventually spew a train. Its darkness unsettled me, raised the hairs on the back of my neck and brought me out in a cold sweat. My legs trembled and the roar of unseen trains made me feel afraid. It seemed that the whispering breeze from the tunnel was taunting me, calling me chicken.

A blast of warm air rippled past and I turned to watch the flight of a chocolate wrapper. More passengers had appeared without me being aware, so fixated had I been on the pitch black hole. Moments later the train sped into the station.

All day I rode the underground, switching lines, exiting only for toilet breaks or to get something to eat and drink. I ate junk from vendor stalls and drank bottles of fizz, listened to buskers playing for change. Some were good, some not so. I stood and watched one guy playing an acoustic guitar. He was great, better than many I've heard on the radio. The words he sang entered my mind moments before he voiced them. I watched the long nails of his right hand plucking the strings and knew which they would go for next, heard the note before it was struck. The short-nailed fingers of his left transferred fluidly from one chord to another, and I found my fingers emulating the movement. Perhaps foolishly, I threw a fiver in the unzipped guitar case. He stopped playing at once and snatched it from the scattering of copper.

"Cheers mate," he said. "You play?"

"Not sure," I mumbled back, and he formed a puzzled expression.

"You've the nails for it." He tipped his eyes in the direction of my right hand.

I walked off without another word, contemplating the long nails, his music fading as I increased the distance between us, the fingers of my left hand dancing over invisible strings, as my mind carried the tune that I'd left in the distant tunnel. If I do play, I could always do that to get by, I thought, as I stepped onto yet another train with no idea where it was heading.

While I rode, I recognised the names of tourist destinations that I had no intention of visiting: Covent Garden, Westminster, St Paul's, Marble Arch, Tower Hill. I realised at that point that my mind wasn't completely gone, only my memories. As I looked around at people in the carriage, I grew envious of the fact that they had a destination; they knew where they were going, and they were going there for a reason. As the train pulled away from the station of London Bridge, I decided I would exit at the next stop and pick somewhere, anywhere, select an actual destination just to feel normal.

Turned out the next station was Waterloo. So I left the underground and I've not been back down there since. Don't know if it means anything, but the black tunnels fill me with dread. Claustrophobia maybe. Don't think I could have picked a busier place than Waterloo. It was heaving, and there were so many platforms to choose from. I now know that Waterloo is Britain's busiest passenger railway station. I walked past the gates to the platforms, stopping at the ones that had trains waiting. I looked at the names of places they dropped off at. Didn't want to head for the end of the line; that just felt too final. In the end, I settled on a place called Brookwood, for no other reason than the name appealed to me.

Brookwood station turned out to be small, as expected. I had hoped to find a bed and breakfast close by, but there wasn't one. It was already colder than earlier in the day, and I could tell it would get colder still. Crossing the main road, navigating a couple of side streets, I came across a canal. Brookwood, I quickly realised, is a narrow village that's held in check like a plant in a pot, train tracks to one side and a canal to the other. Its boundaries are limited. For some reason, I found that comforting; I still do. A few scattered lights twinkled through trees beyond the canal, and roused my curiosity. After crossing a bridge, I walked up a small tarmac track that weaved through woodland.

I discovered houses hidden amongst the trees. Massive, their gardens like small parks. I clambered over the fence of one, and dropped into a garden that appeared to be a continuation of the woodland I'd just left, the fence more of a boundary marker than a transition between private and public property. Tripping over bramble and scratching by holly, I made my way to a large garden shed that was fortunately unlocked. And there, under some old towels that stank of dog, I settled for the night.

* * *

Shit!

I almost knock over the pint as I kick the table. Nicky looks up, but then turns back to Arthur.

Shit!

That can't be...

Fuck!

Heart racing, mind buzzing, hands trembling, a fizz in the veins of my neck, I snap closed the cover of the journal. I can't read any more, not right now. I can practically smell the musty, moulding leaves on the ground in that woodland. I can see the silk-black water in the canal, a frosty moon gleaming on its unwavering surface. Hear a train trundling away from the station to my rear. I felt the damp wood of the fence as I clambered over, the scratch of bramble on my shins, the scrape of holly on my scalp. I can practically taste the fustiness of old towels that stink of dog as I think of settling down to sleep on the gritty floor of a shed full of gardening equipment. It all feels so real.

Is it real?

What is real?

I don't know if it's memory returning, or just my imagination absorbing so readily the words I've just read. It's the dream I had earlier today, though; that's the worst thing. The rape. Running away along the towpath of a canal. It can't be coincidence; it must be memory.

CHAPTER

9

Why did I choose nursing as a career? The curse shouts in my head, as the alarm rings out its rude rasp. Groaning with resignation I slam it into silent submission, and with my head pounding with the after effects of too much wine, I look at the curtains and the glimmer of amber light that highlights their edge. *Holiday. I put in a week's holiday.* Tears come to my eyes as I remember why, as I remember, and as I wonder where Tom is, as I hope he is safe.

I recall too that Kaitlyn stayed the night.

Kaitlyn's not working for the next two days, and she's going to keep pressing me to talk. Sinking into the pillow, groaning, looking up at the ceiling, I wonder how much to tell her. She knows I lived with my Gran through my teenage years, knows my parents are both dead, but she doesn't know all of it. She doesn't know how much it still disturbs my sleep, how I still find it hard to settle at night in an empty house, that it's the reason I used to volunteer to work nights so often. She doesn't know how good Tom has been for me. After being assaulted on the woodland lane I did wonder if I'd ever trust a man enough to get close. Kaitlyn doesn't need to know about that either; it's private. It is in the past. It's something I yearn to forget, and the fewer people that know about it, the easier it is to pretend it never happened. I can't forget it altogether though, as much as I wish I could. If Tom genuinely can't recall his past, and the bigger part of me believes he genuinely can't, I partially envy him his curse.

I'll show Kaitlyn the research I did. Maybe then she'll understand. Maybe then she'll be the supportive friend I know she can be. Hopefully then she'll stop trying to fill my mind with doubts about Tom. I've doubts enough of my own, I don't need her adding to them.

The recurring image of my dad clutching his stomach after tussling with the burglar enters my mind. I'm ten years of age in this memory, and overwhelmed with shock as I watch the hooded man escape through the kitchen window while my dad collapses to the hallway floor.

I could do without revisiting that memory right now.

Why did I not set the alarm to a later time? Or better still, why didn't I turn it off altogether? I'd still be asleep instead of reliving this awful memory.

As is the way with memory or dreams, the timeline mixes up. I'm now thinking of the moment before he fell. Dad is yelling, *get out! Just get out!* I'm standing on the bottom step, wearing the new pyjamas I'd had for Christmas, clutching a neglected old teddy bear to my chest, tears of confusion rolling down my cheeks. *Go back to bed,* he yelled when he spotted me sloping down the steps, rubbing the sleep from my eyes. *Back up to bed. NOW,* loud enough to make the hallway mirror rattle. Then he's on the floor. I see the pool of blood expanding, and hear the shrill blast of Mum's scream as she pushes me aside. I stare at it, confused, and listen to Mum in the hallway, frantic, torn between asking for an ambulance and asking for the police. It all seems so clear, but I'm certain my adult mind fills in the blanks. After the research I've done, I really do wonder just how much we can trust our memories.

Being with Tom helps me get through the night.

I'll get no more sleep. Not now. Not now that the images of the past I'd rather forget have stolen unbidden into my head. If mum had been stronger, it might not have been so bad. The memory might not haunt me as it does. Three years of drinking herself into oblivion. Three years of me preparing food for us, and doing the shopping, and the cleaning. Cleaning her, cleaning up her vomit, helping her into a bath and fresh clothes. Going to live with Gran in the end, when Mum could no longer hide the neglect from her.

Two years later Mum took the overdose, and at the age of fifteen I inherited a house I didn't want, a house where blood had pooled in the hallway, where empty vodka bottles and tablet containers had collected in the bedroom. When the solicitors had done all the legal necessities, Gran helped me to sell the house and invest the money for my future.

"Sorry, Mum. Sorry that Gran wouldn't let me stay. Sorry I couldn't help you to get better."

I couldn't tell Gran about the assault on the lane. I could have told Mum, but she was no longer around.

I force images of Tom into my mind, picturing the time when we met. I use them as a barrier, to block the pain-filled memories. My twenty-first birthday night out was supposed to have been just a quiet drink with Kaitlyn, the only friend I'd made from all the trainee nurses, the only one who knew that Gran had died six months earlier, the only one who knew I had nobody else to celebrate with. She knew I had money too, knew that I was the only trainee nurse with her own flat, bought and paid for, with plenty of money in the bank to spare. Two houses in Surrey generate rather a lot of collateral. She constantly reminded me to keep quiet about my wealth, especially when it came to guys. Not that I needed her advice on that score; I'd have kept it quiet anyway. She always insisted on standing her round too. Still does, though it's more

Costa than cocktail of late.

She's a good friend. Gorgeous looks. But Tom fancied me, not her, no idea why: my nose is too big, my teeth aren't straight, and well, I'm no oil painting. That night, I pretended that I thought he'd been looking at Kaitlyn, pretended that I thought he'd been singing to her. I knew he hadn't been. He'd looked straight into my eyes, even winked at one point. And then he embarrassed the hell out of me by singing 'Angel' directly at me, directing the words to me in particular. He'd looked familiar, but I shook away the feeling. I'd never met him before, or so I'd thought. When we talked during his break, though, he looked at me with the ease of someone who knew me. Seven months back I found out he did, sort of. I recall thinking at the time: *maybe he's just the kind of person who's naturally relaxed in another's company.*

Tom's past may be a mystery, but his present is now an open book; it just has one or two pages missing.

CHAPTER

10

Sheffield city centre is not what I expected. I don't see anything that sparks any memories, which isn't much of a surprise, partly because a good deal of it looks to be newly constructed. Leaving the car behind at The Foundry, I travelled in on a modern tramline that runs from the out-of-town shopping mall to the heart of the city. The contrast of old and new reminds me of my life: elements of it forgotten and abandoned. Nobody cares, and as I feel the weight of the black notebook in my pocket, I wonder if I should truly care about my past. If fifty-one weeks of the year are perfect, why worry about the remaining small portion?

Every young woman I see, every female that catches my eye, reminds me why I should worry. Each and every one of them prevents me from forgetting the dream – *more like a nightmare* – from forgetting the possibility that I might have raped someone in a woodland lane that slopes towards a canal towpath that's dark with overhanging trees. I don't feel like a rapist, but I don't feel like a guitarist either and can't help thinking, *is that what I do? Do I disappear for one week of the year, overcome with an irresistible urge to commit some despicable act? What if that isn't the half of it?*

I'm here now, and I could just walk away from the library. I don't. Instead, I stand there for many minutes, looking up steps that are dished from years of use, questioning whether I should actually pursue this course of enquiry. I could forget it, wait out the week, assuming events transpire as the journal suggests. I could refuse to read another word of it and go back to Surrey, go back to Penny-in-Brookwood, empty handed, empty headed, none-the-wiser.

With a heavy sigh I resign myself to discovering what I will and force my legs to climb the steps. Pulling open a heavy door, I enter the old building and inhale the aroma of time, the peculiar mustiness of so many books in which memories both actual and invented have been written down.

Not quite ready to commit to this venture, I head for the local history section. Perhaps browsing through information on this city will give birth to a memory, assuming that is, that this city is where my memories were formed. *Maybe this place was just a random selection out of many that I could have chosen across the entire country. Maybe this place was just a chance selection, picked like a chocolate from a box with no contents card, just a random place to commit some despicable act before returning to a life of normality with Penny-in-Brookwood.*

After an hour's browsing, learning facts such as Sheffield being the birthplace of stainless steel in 1913, and that it has more trees per person than any other city in Europe – *And my specialist subject is… certainly not the first twenty years of my life* – I give up trying to trigger memories and head for the desk. Two assistants stand behind the counter, one of them young and pretty, an accommodating *may-I-help-you-smile* on her face, the other more elderly and certainly beyond the best years of her life as far as looks are concerned. The older one is busy, her attention fixed on a computer. The expression on her face has a fixed message of *bugger-off-and-ask-somebody-else* about it.

"Is it possible to look at old newspapers?" I ask, part of me hoping the answer will be no.

The tired-looking middle-aged woman does not look up straight away. She focuses on the task at hand, adjusting her glasses and casting a quick glance to the unoccupied woman to her left. While I wait for her to finish whatever it is she's occupied with, I force my eyes to look straight ahead, to not divert to the young woman standing next to her, pretending I'm not remotely aware that she is clearly not engaged in any activity.

Eventually the assistant I'm waiting for does look up. "Any particular one?" She sounds slightly irritated.

Not surprisingly, no title comes to mind.

"Whichever paper it is that would be most likely to carry local news."

My throat feels dry. I envisage her knowing exactly why I want to look at local news. I imagine that she knows the reason why I've asked her rather than the younger and prettier colleague.

You look like a rapist! As the phrase enters my thoughts, it echoes with reverb, in her voice, somewhat like an effect in a low-budget movie. I still feel petrified to glance to the side for fear of receiving the brand of pervert just for looking in her direction. I feel like walking, but as the young woman moves away from the counter a waft of her fragrance fills me with lure-like warmth. It persuades me to stay put. If I am… if I am a rapist, I should find out for sure.

"The Star would likely be your best bet, or the Sheffield Telegraph." The librarian adjusts her glasses and casts a glance into the far reaches of the room. Something in the direction the young woman went causes her to frown slightly and give a subtle shake of her head. She looks back at me, forcing her features into an expression of never-mind. "How far back are you wanting to go, exactly?"

"Possibly nine years, maybe ten. I'm interested in papers from this date through to the end of January, for each year."

She casts me an indulgent smile. I imagine she's thinking of the task of rifling through years' worth of newspapers in search of the ones I'm after. I imagine her having a photographic memory, her seeing in her mind the front page of each and of each one of them having a headline that reports an unsolved rape or mugging or worse.

Her eyes flick to the side and I cast my gaze in the opposite direction as the sweet and musky fragrance hits me. "What's Keith looking for this time?" She questions, keeping her voice low.

"Photoshop," is the answer given, whatever that is. "Something to do with altering images on computers," the young woman adds, her voice indicating that she knows as much about the subject as I do.

With raised eyebrows, the woman serving me shakes her head. "Sorry," she says, adjusting her glasses to once again focus on me. "Keith's a regular here." The slight grimace tells me he's not exactly a welcome one. "Ten years…?" Rhetorical. "The past two years or so is no problem; it's accessible online. Anything older will be on microfilm, but you'll need to book a viewer."

Without waiting for my answer, she immediately opens a logbook and runs her finger down a list of entries. "Quicker than the computer," she says, as if I had been about to ask. She throws the out-dated computer a scowl of disapproval.

Using the opportunity to look behind me, I spot an awkward looking chap who's struggling to carry a pile of books, a shopping bag hooked over his arm that looks more like something an old lady would carry. *At least I look normal,* I think, *even if I'm not.* Quite unexpectedly, I feel sorry for the guy and wonder what it is about him that irritates the women behind the counter. *What's his story?* I wonder, huffing inside at the fact that I don't yet know my own.

"We have a slot two days from now, 3pm, would you like me to book it for you?"

Do I? Really, do I want to search old papers looking for rapes and muggings, scanning for burglaries or even murders that have occurred in January? Do I really want the look of disapproval that Keith chap got? And if I do find anything, if it's not been solved, there's no saying for certain I was responsible. There's probably some crime listed for every day of the week in a city this size; if not this city, then some other. And, there's genuinely no evidence that I actually do come here every year.

"Sir…?"

"Sorry… No… No, I'll leave it, thanks. Sorry to waste your time."

The best way of getting to the bottom of this, I decide, heading back to the tram stop, is to read the rest of that journal.

CHAPTER

1 1

Kaitlyn looks at me expectantly as I place a cup of coffee on the coaster and sit on the very edge of the comfy chair opposite her. Where she lounges, I sit upright and stiff with tension. I glance at the frame that normally holds my favourite picture of Tom, and remember that I left it face down so I would not be reminded that both the picture and the man are missing.

"Despite what I said last night…" Kaitlyn, reaches for the mug of coffee, brings it to within six inches of her mouth, and then puts it back down. "If you don't want to talk about it, then don't."

I glance at the steaming mug set before me, and understand why Kaitlyn picked hers up. Even though it is obviously too hot to drink, my arm is itching to do the same. Such a thing serves as a kind of shield. "It might help… you know, thinking about it … if I do talk about it."

Kaitlyn raises her brow. I'm not quite sure if she's

showing a hint of surprise or satisfaction. "So…" she begins, taking her time over the phrasing. "He goes off on some magical mystery adventure for a week, every January?"

The bunch of my lips is enough to make Kaitlyn lift her hands in a show of silent apology. My subtle nod indicates that her summary is reasonably accurate, despite the unwelcome sarcasm.

"And he's done this every year since moving in with you?"

A nod suffices.

"And before that?"

"Don't know." I pick up the mug. It's still too hot, but I hold onto it all the same. "Tom doesn't remember ever doing it, so he can't say if he disappeared or not before moving in with me." I lean back into the embrace of cushions, giving Kaitlyn the opportunity to say something along the lines of *so he says*. She says nothing, simply picks up her own coffee.

"The year before he moved in though, we had a date arranged and he didn't turn up. It was in January, same week as this. Wouldn't have remembered, but I'd swapped with Kelly and worked her nights so that I could go on that date. Recalling that, I checked back on the ward rotas when my suspicions first got roused. Anyway, that night I couldn't get hold of him. He claimed our date had slipped his mind. I'd worked the rest of the week. I wasn't happy, but a week had passed, so I let it slide."

Kaitlyn probes her cheek with her tongue. It's so obvious how much she's carefully selecting her words that I almost smirk.

"I still find it hard to accept that you believe him."

"That he can't remember disappearing…?" I waver the fingers of my free hand and form an expression that's become a universal spoken language between us, an expression that indicates a kind of *yes and no*. "It's not so much that I do, as that the rest of the time things are so good that I really want to. The time we spend together, the things we do, the way we are; there's never been anything to make me doubt him. And there's something else too, something linked to it that he confessed to, almost a year and a half back."

Sliding deeper into the seat, Kaitlyn seemingly readies herself for the revelation. I take a big gulp of my coffee unsure what the reaction is going to be, but ready to finally share the information nonetheless.

"Tom can't remember anything about the first twenty years of his life."

"What!!?"

If Kaitlyn had taken a slurp of coffee as I told her that, she'd have likely sprayed it all over me. As it is, both her mouth and her eyes are wide with disbelief.

"And you believe that, too?"

She shakes her head as I shrug my shoulders. If the

tables were reversed, I'd likely be saying the same. "I didn't believe it, initially. Then I did, as he spoke about it. Then I didn't. He's never said much about his past since the day we met. I just suspected that there were things he wanted to forget, or that he had a past not worth mentioning. I've given him similar responses when he's asked about my past. So, as far as believing him, I've wavered from one to the other, finally siding with belief. After the research I've done, I'm more convinced."

"But not totally?"

"Not one-hundred per cent, no; I'm not completely stupid."

I can see the cogs turning behind Kaitlyn's expression as she takes a sip of her coffee. "What's this research then?"

"It's to do with memory loss. I'll show you later."

Kaitlyn gives me a look that says she can take it or leave it. "So, why hasn't he looked into his past? You know, tried to find out?"

"He doesn't know who he is."

Kaitlyn scowls at that. "I thought you meant he just didn't remember certain things, not that he had no identity… He doesn't remember anything?"

"Nothing personal."

"But if he has no identity, that must mean he has no driving licence…? Yet he drives."

I nod, leaving that as a blank to fill her in on later.

Now is not the right time for more revelations.

"…And no passport. So that time I went with you to Lanzarote in his place wasn't because he was sick. You told me he'd paid for his half and then couldn't go."

I play my *sorry* card in the form of a grimace, which Kaitlyn replies to with pursed lips of *not happy*. "I paid for his ticket as a surprise. I didn't think to ask him if he'd got a passport, and this is before I knew about, you know… him not knowing who he was. He suggested taking you instead, rather than rush to get a passport, said he had commitments he couldn't drop. It made sense at the time. The only reason I didn't tell you was because I knew you'd feel uncomfortable about the money, that you wouldn't be happy about me paying, and you wouldn't have money to spare to pay for yourself."

"Too right I wouldn't have been happy… Bloody hell, Pen. Well I'm paying you back."

"No, you're not…"

Silence falls on the room for a moment, as we both finish our coffee. I'm contemplating Kaitlyn trying to pay for the holiday months from now, and she's probably envisioning my refusal.

"He could have tried the police. Missing persons, whatever."

"Tom said he was scared of discovering he was someone who's done something bad. Rather be a free person with no identity than a jailed person with an identity but no memory. Said he kind of just got used to the not knowing. Shelved it and got on with his life as best he could."

Again Kaitlyn shakes her head and throws me a look of disapproval. "And that didn't scare you?"

"A bit." Screwing my mouth, I shrug and reflect on the possibility of him having a shady past that he knows nothing of, or of knowing but not letting on about it. "Had I learned of it when we'd first met, of course I'd have walked away. Heck, I'd have run. We've lived together these past years though, and I know him. That makes a big difference. Tom is a good guy. He's never done anything to make me doubt it."

"I can't believe this. I've known Tom as long as you have, and yet I don't know him at all."

No you haven't, I silently argue. *I met him before you did, sort of.* Something else he confessed to, only last March.

"So, when did it come to light then, this missing twenty years?"

"May 2014. I wanted to go on holiday, fancied Barcelona for my twenty-fifth birthday. Tom's doing, that I fancy going there I mean, from when he started covering George Ezra's tracks." A smile creeps onto my face, as I picture and hear in my mind the more up to date music he now sings. He still thinks

Aerosmith's *Angel* is my favourite of his, but that song makes me sad now that I know of his past. I much prefer his rendition of Ezra's Barcelona. His voice melts me when he sings that one.

"He does sing Barcelona well." Kaitlyn throws me a half-hearted smile. "I like the Jake Bugg stuff he sings though, especially that Seen It All song."

The Jake Bugg stuff worries me, reminds me that he might be from somewhere dodgy, *where everyone has a knife.* "Anyway, all this is beside the point, my wanting to go to Barcelona started the argument. He has no passport and no way of getting one, but at that point he couldn't admit to that, which left me wondering why. Among other things, I accused him of not loving me. Then I started ranting about stuff other than the holiday, like how I thought we'd have got engaged by now, and why was he holding back, because I thought we would have at least discussed the possibility of one day getting married. He said he could think of nothing he'd rather do. Well, to cut a long story short, eventually he broke down in tears – I mean real wracking, gut-wrenching sobs. He blathered on, not making any real sense, saying he wanted to ask me to marry him, but that he couldn't, that he was afraid. Eventually, he came out with the real reason."

Kaitlyn raises her brow, and I don't really know if I can read from her expression what she's actually thinking. So I simply shrug, as if to say, *over to you.*

"As far as I can see, it doesn't matter whether this missing memory business is true or not, Pen. This missing twenty years." Kaitlin is getting serious now. I can see it in her expression and in her posture as she places the empty mug on the coffee table and leans towards me, perched on the edge of the chair. "If this memory issue is not true, why is Tom saying it is? What's he hiding? If it is true…" She blows a breath of air and shakes her head. "If it is, it could… He could be anyone. He could be a criminal, a… a nutter, a thug, a rapist, anything!"

I really feel like ranting at her, arguing against her, but I keep my thoughts to my self.

He isn't a rapist. I think, clenching my jaw, trapping the words. *He's quite the opposite.*

CHAPTER

1 2

I can't quite believe how eager I am to get back to reading the journal. I don't recall one solitary title of any book that I might have ever read, but I get the feeling that I have enjoyed reading in the past. And, just as one would with a novel, I'm drawn to discovering what is going to happen next to the principal character of my current read. I'm doubly invested in that character, though. Not surprisingly really, for that character is yours truly. Therein, I am both keen and yet filled with trepidation as I rush through the bar, waving a quick hello to the landlord before I head up the back stairs to my room.

Visiting the library had been a waste of time. I did find something strangely comforting about the place though. All those stories, I suppose, stories about people and their lives. It was time I should have spent here though, reading the very book that does contain answers, the book that contains the story of my life. Just because I dreamt about a rape doesn't mean that I am a rapist, and no report in an old newspaper will clarify it either way.

Key wavering in my hand, I unlock the door. Switch the kettle on. Make a cuppa and settle down to dive into the text. A phrase comes to mind as I open the embossed lilac cover: *unreliable narrator.* Stroking my cheek in contemplation, I then wonder, *how much can I trust the words written in here?* If the text is to be truly believed, that means Penelope is looking in this book too, reading all that has been written down. There was even a page ripped out because she supposedly objected to something that had been mentioned. Is it therefore going to be a full and accurate disclosure?

Flicking the collection of pages against my thumb, I expect to see the word LIE flash across a random page: LIE in big loopy strokes of red marker pen. I note that every page has been written on. That's quite a lot of words, but then he did have a full year... Correction, I had a full year to write it. The very idea that I wrote this feels ridiculous. There is no evidence to prove that I did, but there's none proving that I didn't either. I doubt there's an entry for every day of the past year. There aren't enough pages. Sure enough, I see gaps between the dated entries. I also know it's a story without an end. The end is hopefully for me to write or at the very least discover while I am here. Not an end, that would mean death if it were to be the end of my story. A satisfactory conclusion is what I'm looking to write: a resolution to the instigating catalyst of the tale. There's no beginning either. Can't help but let out a huff of amusement at that. Every story needs a beginning, middle and end. This one I'm about to dive back into is only the middle; I'm meant to discover its extremities. Then again, at what point should a story begin?

* * *

2nd February 2015.

Two days of writing in a row. Not sure I'll keep up this kind of pace, but I have to say this writing lark is quite addictive. I might just keep it up and write an actual proper story from the beginning, a story that I can invent in the knowledge that I'm not lying to myself.

So, I've stumbled upon a place called Brookwood, Surrey, and I'm living in this shed. Thin wooden walls do little to keep out the cold, but it was better than being outdoors. I only ever saw an elderly lady come and go from the house. Frail looking, with a slight stoop to her back, she favoured one leg more than the other, which gave the appearance that she almost walked sideways.

Each day of those two weeks, she'd exit the house, lock the door, give a firm shake on the handle, and head off down the drive. I guessed that she was likely shopping or visiting friends, or both. When she went shopping is when I went shopping, primarily for something to eat. I always went for something that steamed with heat, and that was as cheap as I could find.

The money in my pocket wasn't going to last forever and I soon discovered it isn't easy to find somewhere warm to shelter that is also free. The library served me well in that regard, and I soon discovered a love of reading. I haven't a clue if it's always been the case but I easily got through most books in a day. One time when I put a half-finished thick volume on the shelf the librarian said, "why not take it home? I can make you a member, if you like?" Naturally, I declined. Other than having no ID and no address, the library was the best place to build up the heat I would need to get me through the night. Having the right to take a book away would have felt like I had less of a right to stay.

Just over three weeks passed by in that fashion. The old dear rigorously checking the lock on the door, me heading to the café for a cuppa, then off to the library for a warm, leaving at lunch for a bag of chips (nice fat steaming chunks of potato, not the skinny fries you get in fast food joints. Wrapped in paper, they warmed my hands as well as my gut), then back to the library where I stayed until closing. I still had no idea where I'd come from, and no idea where to go, so I had no issue with living the same day over and over. The lack of variance in my days made living the lives of others through all those books all the more magical.

Anyway, that was that, until one night I sneaked back into the shed and discovered something unusual: an aroma. The damp and musky dog stink had been partially masked with a much more pleasant fragrance. The lights were all out in the house. I'd checked, as always, before sneaking into the garden. Didn't want to give the old dear a heart attack, and more importantly, I didn't want her ringing the police to report an intruder. Opening the shed door and allowing moonlight to enter, the whiteness of the duvet was almost blinding. It didn't occur to me at first that it looked too clean and fresh to be stored in a shed with the same disregard as old dog-towels. I just thought lucky me: lucky that I make myself scarce in the daytime, lucky that my nights are now going to be warmer.

It was only when I unrolled the duvet that I saw the flask and the flashlight and the note.

My initial instinct was to scarper. I didn't. I opened the flask and almost melted at the rippling fragrance of tomato soup, its hot dampness coating my face with moisture as I drew the delicious smell into my nose. After closing out the cold night, slurping the soup while wrapped in the clean duvet, I finally turned the flashlight onto the note.

I'm not going to tell you what it said.

I'm not going to tell you, because I still have it. I'm going to glue it on the next page. Hopefully, you might remember when you first received it.

You never know, it might spark something.

* * *

My hand partially curls the page in anticipation of turning it over. I'm itching to look at that note, but I don't. I close the journal. It's gone lunchtime and, inspired by what I've just read, I find I'm craving food: chips to be exact: big fat greasy fluffy on the inside, crisp yellow on the outside, steaming chunks of potato. My tongue fizzes in anticipation of the heat and the lashing of salt and vinegar that I'm going to coat them in. The desire, the hunger, the anticipation of eating this food shoots my mind to sitting in a library, looking at the clock on the wall and waiting for the time I will set out to eat something hot and satisfying. It feels like returning memory, but I've just read about doing this very thing in the journal, so I can't be certain.

Just a glance at the note…

No.

I want to come back to that part.

If memory floods into my mind upon looking at the note, I want to be in a position where I can give the subsequent writing my full attention. Twenty or thirty minutes aren't going to hurt any; the journal isn't going anywhere and, until I discover something concrete, nor am I.

Taking a moment to ponder what I've just read, I find it hard to believe that I might have done the despicable act I earlier feared, but a portion of dread remains all the same. I guess I'll find out something, hopefully trigger memories the more I read.

A realisation strikes me: the writing style in the journal has changed. It no longer has the note-like quality of the initial pages; it now reads more like a novel. It's hardly surprising that I would want to emulate the books that I've supposedly read. Maybe I began to enjoy writing it. I imagine it was quite cathartic. Thinking about it, writing something in a boring style would likely be just as tedious as reading something in a boring style.

CHAPTER

1 3

The landlord – a man so big of gut that I secretly name him landlard – gave me directions to a chip-shop that, while not the closest, is supposedly the best in the area. And, as I drive away from Popple Street chippy, fully satisfied and fit to burst with a gut-full of hot greasy potato, I give the landlard a mental nod of confirmation.

I'm eager to get back to the journal but I drive at a steady speed, taking in the surroundings, my eye constantly snagged by the hill, rising to my left, where I woke in the car. I can't help thinking that something drew me to this place. I wonder if I come here every year, or do I go to different places. The not knowing feels like a physical part of me is missing, somewhat like the outside is intact, but someone has scooped out a portion of my centre. Within me there is hollowness: a hole into which I could just collapse at any moment.

Bringing my attention back to the surroundings,

my eyes are drawn to the right, away from the hill, to a railway track that runs parallel to the road. For the most part it is hidden from view, but it remains evident because of the building style of the walls and of the stud-riveted steel panels along its length where pedestrian bridges span its width. Something does not always have to be seen for one to know it is there. Just like my memories, clues point to the existence of the unseen railway track. There are clues everywhere; some are simply more elusive than others. Beyond the railway track towers a large building constructed from black corrugated metal. A narrow road to the side catches my eye and causes a feeling of fear to flutter my heart and flip my gut. Looking in the mirror and seeing no traffic behind, I slow to a barely perceptible crawl.

A tremor chills the back of my neck as I look down the road. It drops steeply, diving under the railway tracks that have been rendered visible by a patch of land that now shows only the scar of what once stood there. Weeds sprout from gaps in the brickwork and fly-tipping litters the pavements. The entrance to what is surely a tunnel, and not a bridge as I first suspected, looks darker than a moonless night. Despite the brightness of this cold crisp day, very little light penetrates the depth. Imagined hammers thump in my mind as I look once more to the massive black-clad building on the right, the corrugated metal is peeled back in places like makeshift doors, while higher up it is rusted right through, showing a glimpse of sky. My heart pounds to triple its prior beat as I take in the puddle that spans the entire width of the road. Water drips from a rusty patch in a wide pipe that skirts the top of the wall and disappears into the corrugated black cloak of the ominous building that towers up on the right. With steady timing, the drips splash into the puddle, distorting the black reflection of the void beyond.

Two pigeons fly from the mouth of the tunnel, startling me, their wings clattering.

I don't know if I've seen this steep narrow road before, or the frightful looking tunnel into which it descends. I am likely not the only one who has looked upon it. Then again it would be easily missed by anyone driving along at a normal pace with a definite destination in mind.

A man looking for ghosts is likely to see them whether they are real or not, I assure myself.

If I'm going to find answers, I need to carry on reading that journal. If I learn nothing else, at least I'll know the middle of my own story.

I close my eyes, take a big breath, and drive on, my heart still clattering like the wings of those pigeons.

The note has the appearance of having been carried in a back pocket for years and then ironed before being taped to this page of the journal. It's stained with denim blue along the lines of creases that have furred edges, indicating that it has been unfolded and then re-folded on many occasions. *Please don't lose the note*, the writing requests, before stating that I have kept it to remind me how kind some people can be when they spot someone in need. I re-read it several times, before continuing reading the next entry.

* * *

Dear Man in my shed,

I hope these gifts make your stay more comfortable. I assume you're not dangerous, because you've been here for at least two weeks, and all you appear to do is sleep in there. All the same, I still feel I'm taking a bit of a risk. Please don't prove me to be an old fool. I could do with a gardener/odd-job man. Perhaps we could come to an arrangement.

Best, P. Gaskell

The morning after finding this note, I knocked on the door to the house. I'd still not seen anyone other than the old lady, and I assumed that she was the P. Gaskell that had written the note. It was possible that someone else lived in the house, but somehow I didn't think so. I felt a little trepidation, but if she had intended to call the police, she would have done so before going to the trouble of providing me with soup and a duvet.

It took an age for her to get to the door, and I assumed the old dear had changed her mind. As you can probably gather from the note, she is a bit of a character. "Ah! The shed dweller," she said, trying her best to stop a smirk from rising.

I mumbled something about finding the note, and about wondering what kind of arrangement she had in mind. She invited me in to discuss terms over a cup of tea, which turned out to be several mugs and a bacon-butty.

When she asked for my name and I said it was Tom, she gave me that look that people give when they are anticipating and waiting for more. Rather than tell her I didn't know my surname, I said: *if you're waiting for my surname, I'd rather not say.* She gave me a questioning glare, as if trying to read me, and pursed her lips as if realising that I'd been written in a foreign language.

"Well," she said. She then paused for what seemed an age, as if going over in her mind what she planned to say before actually saying it. She then continued and, to the best of my knowledge, said something like, "I'd rather you not use my surname either, if I'm honest; makes me feel damn old being called Mrs Gaskell, as if I don't get enough of a reminder from my aching joints. But if I'm going to be employing you, I cannot be having you calling me Pauline within earshot of anyone else. They will think I've gone soft. In conjunction, because people have certain expectations of me, they will become suspicious if I tell them I know you only as Tom. As you are going to be in my employ as a gardener, I propose we refer to you as Tom Gardener. After all, that is how surnames came into being in the first instance."

So, that's how the name of Gardener came about. I wonder if you've remembered my real surname. Write it down if you have.

As Pauline (a name I still only use for her when nobody else is in ear shot) got to know me, she said she was impressed with my "exuberant attitude to work" (her words not mine). She balanced the compliment by saying it went someway towards compensating "my complete lack of knowledge in regard to flora" (also her words). Despite that lack of knowledge - something she set out to rectify - she recommended me to others, all who thought it highly delightful to have a gardener that was named Gardener.

That night, Pauline allowed me to move into the smallest bedroom in the house, the four larger unoccupied rooms being reserved for special guests that never came. Over a number of weeks I discovered that Pauline had been a headmistress in a private school. Her husband had been something big in engineering, and had travelled the world as a result, leaving her for the most part a single woman. Her father had been someone high up in government, and when she lived abroad as a young girl they'd had servants. They had a son quite late in life. He married and had a son of his own. The grandson had lived with Pauline for the years he had attended university. She never elaborated on the reason, but he had used the same small room that I used, and judging by the things he left behind (Tee-shirts and posters with various slogans), I get the impression that he did not get along with his parents. Anyway, Pauline's son lives in Scotland (she thinks). She hasn't seen or heard of him for over twenty years. Her grandson lives in Canada, where he moved to after graduating two years before I happened to be discovered in her shed.

Pauline wouldn't tell me what had alerted her to the fact that I was staying in her shed. She merely tapped her nose when I asked, and said: I have my ways, and a lady should never be pressed into revealing her ways. Two days later, she admitted that she often sat in the dark in an upstairs room that faced the garden, watching bats and owls that flew over the lane that led to the canal. She had watched as I sneaked back into the shed each and every night. She also admitted to watching me visit the library and the chip shop. When she'd finally come to the conclusion that I was no threat, she decided to offer me work.

Pauline only ever paid me with food and lodgings. Not one penny has ever passed from her palm to mine. But as I gathered customers from amongst her friends (or associates, as she refers to them) I did start to make a reasonable income, all cash-in-hand, for obvious reasons.

Her grandson had left a selection of clothes in the room and they did me for the early weeks. I didn't know if I had a style of my own, so I temporarily adopted his. Over the years I've naturally progressed away from that style, but the gardening and gigging tends to keep me casual for the most part. My favourite item of clothing is a leather coat that I saved for after buying a guitar. Have I mentioned buying the guitar? I think saving hard for something, working hard to earn that money, makes the purchase all the more satisfying.

Have I mentioned the gigging? Can't remember that either, and I can't be bothered to read back. Sorry, there may be some repetition as this continues. I've no intention of editing this thing!

So, gigging. After saving for a couple of months, I went in search of an acoustic guitar with the intention of practising enough to see if I could get work playing in bars. Despite having a sense that I knew how to play, it may have just been a fanciful wish. I also didn't have a clue what make of guitar I was shopping for.

I didn't need to know, as it happened, because the guitar I purchased kind of picked me. It sat there on its own, looking beautiful and dark among all the blond wood instruments to either side. As I stood and stared at it, and occasionally picked up the price tag to see if I'd read it correctly, the shop assistant finally approached.

"I see you've taken a fancy to the Tanglewood," he said, and stood by my side for at least ten minutes, also silently admiring the instrument.

"Bit more than I wanted to pay." I glanced at the second hand guitars near the door. My hand closed around the roll of notes in my pocket, all I had to my name. The cost of this beautiful dark-wood guitar would leave me with little more than a fiver in change. In reality it was not all that pricey, there were much more expensive instruments in the shop. No other with the glorious look of tobacco staining, however: a look of wood captured in time.

"Give it a play," the shop assistant suggested, lifting it from the hooks that held it to the wall. "It's of the Crossroads series. Styled on the 1930s guitars that the blues singers of the day would have owned. It has a sound to match."

I held it for a quite a while before even daring to touch the strings, too embarrassed to strum in-case some awful clash of sound proved that I was actually mistaken in the belief that I could play. I glanced several times at the cheaper pre-owned guitars near the door, but I really liked the idea of owning something that was named crossroads. I felt that was exactly where I was. And I could certainly identify with the ethos of the blues. In the end I paid for the guitar without striking a single note. I did hear it though, before handing over the money; the assistant insisted and played a tune for me. I suspect it was more for his benefit than mine.

Turns out I didn't need to practise for long, and I can only guess that I must have been playing for years. My fingers didn't even get slightly sore.

Reflecting on this time and thinking about Pauline's absent son, has made me wonder more than I ever have in the past if my parents are still alive. If they are, do they wonder why they haven't seen me for eight years or more?

Are you with them by any chance? I hope so.

I'm still trying to think of particular instances that might spark memories, and I have to say it's harder than I thought it would be.

There was the time when Pauline persuaded me to join her art class. I think it would be hard to imagine such a collection of eccentrics, most of them retired, all but one of them female, and all of them with interesting tales to tell. The stories they have about the lives they've lived are as varied as the clothes they wear. I didn't attend too frequently. I couldn't draw or paint to save my life, but the main reason was the constant suggestion that I pose for them... naked!

"I've seen him with his shirt off," Liz often said. "When he's been working on my garden."

"But have you seen him in shorts?" Maureen would reply without pause, as if they'd rehearsed what to say.

"We'll pay," one of the others would say.

"I'm not even bothered about drawing," another would add.

And so it would go on, me shaking my head, not really knowing what to say, thinking if this were a group of men and it were a young woman attending, they'd all be branded perverts.

"Difference is, lad," said Arthur - more commonly referred to as Major on account of his always wearing a blazer with polished brass buttons, and his walrus mustache - as if he knew what I was thinking, "they're only teasing. Whereas, if the genders were reversed." He coughed away his thoughts rather than say the actual words, and tipped me a sly wink.

* * *

I close the journal, having read all of February's entries, noting that the regularity of them is already spreading out. In the third week of February, nothing at all had been written.

I can tell that Pauline Gaskell has played an important role in my life. Every single entry that I wrote in February included her or something involving her and the group of friends she referred to as associates.

A chuckle rises in me and bursts into true laughter, as I reflect on some of the passages I've just read. For a moment, it feels like memory returning and a tear trickles down my cheek at the thought.

Strongest of all is the passage that relates to the first gig I apparently did in one of the local pubs. According to the journal, everyone in the art group attended to show their support. I feel I can see them all, cheering me on, my thoughts seemingly stretching beyond the words I've read. A broad smile steals onto my face as I picture Maureen and Liz waving scarves above their heads, Pauline clapping politely and telling them to sit as if they were errant schoolchildren on a class outing. Arthur tipping a glass of brandy and nodding his approval as I sing a song he requested, a song that I had practised all week being as I'd never heard of it.

Is it memory, though?

Or is it invention?

As one would when reading a novel, am I merely filling in blanks and expanding the story beyond that given in the narration?

With nobody to corroborate, I have no way of knowing.

It does make me wonder to what extent memory can actually be trusted.

I also can't help thinking that surely Penny must be more important to me than the elderly folk I now seem to be remembering. What I've so far read of Penny hasn't encouraged the filling in of blanks; it hasn't brought anything to mind that feels like genuine memory. Maybe the memories that are most precious to us are too fixed, set in stone, so to speak, and being less pliable, are not prone to alteration or invention. That very thought makes me think that I am merely expanding on what I've read, that my mind is creating an invented past from the fragments it has been offered.

There is the possibility that I have not yet read enough about Penny. Maybe there is not enough completed of the puzzle to make sense of the picture of her that it will eventually reveal.

CHAPTER

14

I can't believe I let Kaitlyn talk me into hitting the sales. I should be at home, miserably awaiting Tom's return, not out trying to enjoy myself. I can't stand the hustle and bustle of sales at the best of times. On the upside, at least this far into January, the shops are relatively empty of shoppers; on the downside, they're also relatively empty of bargains that are worth bagging. Anything worth having has already gone. It hasn't really taken my mind away from Tom either, as Kaitlyn suggested it would. Guilt weighs me down whenever I stop thinking about him, whenever I smile or dare to even think about laughing. *We won't even talk about it,* she'd claimed, and yet every so often she can't help making a remark that hints towards what she'd really like to say. On more than one occasion I've had to bite my tongue, almost telling her about the time I came close to being raped. I really don't want her to know. I really don't, for Tom's sake more than mine.

"Let's go for a coffee," Kaitlyn suggests, turning to

face me, as we're about to enter yet another shop festooned with garish red posters proclaiming savings that are at best debateable. "All this shopping is getting a little heavy."

She holds up the one tiny bag that contains nothing more than a tube of mascara: the entire haul of our afternoon's trudge around the sales. We both look at the bag and as our eyes reconnect we burst into howls of laughter.

"Come on," she says, threading her arm through mine, reflecting the look of sadness that is surely ingrained in my expression, and rolling her lower lip as a sign of empathy. "My treat. A big slice of cake too, I reckon. Haven't spent anywhere near enough money today."

The laughter is quickly buried under a tumble of guilt and once again I can't help but wonder what Tom is doing right now. A frosty mist floats in the air, the kind that renders roads to black ice. I hope he's safe. Many has been the time he's refused to let me drive to work, his fear of the cold and dark mornings bordering on irrational, my argument that the roads have been gritted, that my car – on his insistence – is wearing its winter boots, making little impression on his concern.

The coffee shop wraps me with comforting warmth and freshly ground aroma the instant Kaitlyn opens the door. I take a look at the last glimmer of daylight beneath a black cloud, and whisper, "stay safe, Tom." Kaitlyn turns to me with a look that tells me she thinks I may have said something. She seemingly accepts my smile as evidence that she heard wrong, and advances to a booth in the plushest depth of the room. Second-hand books line the walls. I note that none of today's customers are reading. *Are you reading, Tom?* I hope he is, and I hope it's making a difference.

While Kaitlyn queues at the counter, I scan the books on the shelf to my right. My eye is drawn to a battered, old-looking volume that's bound in what looks something like pale-denim: scuffed like jeans on the edges and faded towards a yellowish hue. The book has a certain familiarity, so I slide it out. With a huff of ironic humour, I notice it's a copy of 'Great Expectations'. It's The Pears Edition, the very copy that my grandmother owned. I sold most of the contents of her house to a clearance specialist after she passed away. It seems that this book eventually found its way here, ready to fall back into my hands.

A flood of memory rushes my mind as I open the book and inhale a blast of my gran's living room: a strange aromatic mix of rosewater and soot. I'm thirteen years old in this memory and have been living with Gran for around six months. I'm lying on my stomach before the coal fire, and not so much reading this book as flicking through the pages and marvelling at the strange order of the words within randomly selected sentences. *Us two being now alone,* I remember once saying when Gran came into the room. The novel became a favourite of mine. I went through a stage of acting out aspects of the story, pretending that I was Estella, and referred to jacks as knaves when we played rummy. If back then I played the role of Estella, I'm now more in danger of becoming Mrs Haversham. I'm not likely to even make wedding arrangements, though, so it's not very likely that I'll be left with the dust-gathering collection that she had. Tom is determined that he will not marry me until he knows who he is, until he knows himself to be the kind of person he believes I deserve. If his memory doesn't return, the man I love will not marry me. He will continue to hold back. I will be Mrs Haversham, but without the moulding dust gathering wedding paraphernalia.

"What's the book?" Kaitlyn places the tray of cake and frothy coffee on the table and sinks beside me into the depth of the soft leather sofa.

"Great Expectations…" I open the book to the title page where Gran wrote the inscription: *to Penelope, my very own Estella, on your 14th birthday.* "It was Gran's. She gave it to me. Wish I'd kept it, but I forgot all about it when the house was cleared.

"Take it," she says, matter-of-factly, not even glancing around the room to see if anyone is listening.

"I can't do that; it's stealing."

Kaitlyn curls her lip. "It's more yours than theirs, by rights. Besides, who's going to miss a grotty old book like that – no offence. I bet nobody's even picked it up once, all the while it's been here."

"All the same…"

"Give it here." Kaitlyn doesn't actually wait for me to hand the book over, as she snatches it from my grasp and promptly slips it into her handbag. "You can close your mouth, Pen. You haven't stolen it, I have." She traps a wicked smirk in the grip of her teeth, before casting a sly look at the counter. "Nobody's even noticed. I'll give it you later. Call it part-payment for that holiday."

"Put it back." I try to reach into her bag, but she clamps her hand over it.

"Try that again," she says, with a girlish giggle, "and I'll scream that you're trying to steal my purse."

Again the wicked smirk. This time her teeth fail to hold her lips, and it breaks into a broad smile.

"Fine… Fine," I say, holding up a hand of defeat.

Chocolate cake and talking is not a pretty mix. Consequently, for a few moments we enjoy a delightfully sticky period of silence.

The silence is broken when Kaitlyn squirms on the couch, pulls an expression of discomfort, and expels a sound of displeasure that's a blend of tut and a sigh. "I meant to buy an epilator."

"Thought you bought one six months back?"

"Hmmm, I did. Scary incident," she says, throwing a dramatic expression into the mix. "I decided to try epilating my faff, and it got stuck… I'm tugging away, and it's grabbing on for grim death. Ended up having to switch it off at the mains, throw a towel around me, and head for the kitchen for some scissors with it still hanging on."

Kaitlyn rolls her eyes at the laughter I can't quite hold in, my hand shielding a spray of chocolate cake crumb.

"Had to cut it off, didn't I. Spent ages untangling the little wheel thingies with a pair of tweezers, and then discovered the motor had burnt out."

Nothing like laughter to take your mind away from the thing that's been constantly occupying it. Occupying is the correct word for such a thing, though, for that's what it does: it occupies. Returns. Inhabits. Squats. Refuses to leave. The laughter is merely a facade, and when the jollity fades the occupying guilt and hollowness remain. My laughter dies and the tears of laughter quickly sour toward tears of sadness.

"Right, then, Missy." Kaitlyn says, brushing chocolate crumbs from her lap. She passes me a tissue, and offers a warm smile of comfort. "I'd like to know about this research you've done."

"Can't that wait till I get home?" After wiping my

eyes, I give my nose a good blow. "I've got it all printed out."

"Yes, well. I'm not going back to yours, am I. Got work tomorrow. Just give me the summary."

"Alright then." With a heavy sigh, I take a moment to cogitate. "Obviously, it's to do with memory loss. I was just looking for general information, at first, not in depth medical research. But, I found out about a condition called psychogenic amnesia. It's also known as dissociative amnesia. The people who suffer from it don't show any sign of brain damage or neurobiological cause."

"Bloody hell, Pen. I might be a nurse, but don't forget I work in orthopaedics. Neurobiological…? Right, got it… no nerve damage. Go on."

"The research says it's considered the equivalent of a clinical condition known as repressed memory syndrome. It can be brought on as a result of severe stress or psychological trauma. It presents itself in one of two ways: global amnesia, also known as fugue state, in which the sufferer has a sudden loss of personal identity involving extended periods of wandering and confusion."

"Ha! That's my Paul, most Saturdays."

"Do you want to hear this, or not?"

Kaitlyn morphs her face into the grimace that means sorrreeeee. Forcing an emphasised wrinkling of my brow, I carry on.

"This fugue state usually lasts for only a number of days, and the thing that brought it on can be lost from the memory. The other type is called... situation-specific amnesia. It occurs as a result of a severely stressful event. So I got to thinking that maybe Tom is suffering from both. An emotional shock of some sort could have caused him to erase the first twenty years of memories. And as those memories return, for whatever reason, the fugue state could kick in for a week or so. He'd not remember a thing about it if that were the case."

"Sounds like a long stretch to me."

I shrug my shoulders in reply, having already assumed that Kaitlyn would take some convincing. "Not impossible though. Every medical condition has extreme cases. Anyway I followed it up with some psychological research, and Freudian study suggests that this type of amnesia is an act of self-preservation. It's claimed that the alternative could be overwhelming anxiety or even suicide. So, to protect itself the mind blocks unwanted, dangerous memories from entering the consciousness. It's a kind of subconscious self-censorship."

"I think Freud could have done with some self-censorship. Wasn't he obsessed with lads wanting to shag their mothers? Oh dippy pussy complex."

"I'm trying to be serious!"

While Kaitlyn controls her sniggering, I take a

moment to put my thoughts in order. Before continuing, I down the last mouthful of coffee, which has gone cold. "There are actual hormones that come into play: stress hormones. Can't remember the name of them, but they block normal autobiographical memory processing."

I throw Kaitlyn a look that to my mind says you can't argue with science.

"I still say you're stretching the facts to suit the circumstances."

At least she sounds serious now. At least she's not joking, even if she is arguing against me. Maybe that's what I need.

"Okay," Kaitlyn says before pausing a moment, seemingly getting her thoughts in order. "If I understand this right, you're claiming that some kind of traumatic event has made him block all memory of his first twenty years. But, he then begins to remember it, once a year, which causes him to temporarily forget his life with you because of this fugue state. And because that's a temporary state, he eventually remembers you and returns home with no idea why he left in the first place, and with no idea that he actually left at all."

"Is that so hard to believe?"

Kaitlyn huffs a breath ringing with incredulity. "Quite frankly, yes."

"There is more to it, Kait. I knew I should have

waited to show you the paperwork. It explains how these repressed memories can be recovered spontaneously, years or even decades after the event that caused them to be repressed in the first place. It could be unlocked by something as simple as a smell or a taste of something, or even something like an anniversary. I was thinking, what if the anniversary of something began to bring back the repressed memory, but then eventually remembering the actual event pushed the emerging memory away? I think that's a possibility. The people who suffer psychogenic amnesia often lose their biographical memories. As a result, they can't remember their name or their address, and they particularly can't remember the events that led up to the trigger."

"I don't know, Penny. Tom just seems so normal."

I could do without the look of pity, but I choose not to mention it. "That's what's even more convincing. They usually preserve their semantic and procedural memories; they know what things mean, and they remember things they've learned – like playing the guitar for example. They also have the ability to create new memories."

Kaitlyn looks at me for a good length of time, cogs in her mind most obviously turning. "Okay. Let's say this is what's happening to Tom. Surely he'd be better going to see a hypnotist or some kind of therapist than writing in a journal."

"Maybe. If this doesn't work, I'll encourage him to try something like that. The problem is, though, that without corroborative evidence, they can't say for certain which are true repressed memories and which are fabricated false ones."

"And if it does work?" Kaitlyn screws her lips, emphasising her dramatic pause. "If it turns out that this supposed traumatic event is something to do with him being a murderer or something like that, what then?"

"I'll cross that bridge if I get to it. But it won't be anything like that. I know Tom; he's a good guy."

CHAPTER

1 5

I needn't have left the car at The Foundry; the roads are not as slippery as I'd anticipated they would be. Still, there's no better way of taking in one's surroundings than on foot, and standing here, a third of the way up the hill, is a church that looks familiar. That familiarity spawns no actual memory; it just gives me a feeling of... not comfort, exactly... more a sensation of belonging, of being in a place that's not exactly alien. Just slightly further down the hill from the church is a recreational ground that's stepped into two levels, the lower one sports swings and a slide and a roundabout. The upper level is a flat pitch of dark red cinder, marked out for five-a-side football or hockey. Having just walked the entire perimeter, I lean onto the fence surrounding the recreational ground and gaze at the red cinder. Large circles have been etched into its surface. As with the church, the circles claw with the insistence of a memory buried too deep for extraction, and with a feeling of frustration, I continue my climb up the hill.

Standing here, at the exact location where I woke in the car, feeling quite breathless from the climb, watching the lights of commuters' cars heading to a definite destination, I'm filled with envy. Looking at lights glowing in homes near and far, some filtered by coloured curtains, I'm filled with longing.

I hear the laughter of children in a distant street, unseen but heard, calling each other names and kicking a can. *Shouldn't they be in bed?* I think, before realising it's only just turned seven. Such is the trickery of the short days in winter, the cold and the darkness that I absolutely loathe.

What feels like a spark of memory pushes through that loathing and brings with it a twirl of giddy excitement. I suddenly feel the rush of once enjoying nights like this, when windows sparked to life and heavy curtains shut out the night. The feeling has perhaps been inspired by the unseen volume of children enjoying the anonymity of darkness, but I can't help thinking that this was the time I loved as a kid: when grown-ups hid indoors and the world belonged to us. Dusk, when mischief hides in shadows. *Where danger lurks unseen.*

I have a distinct feeling that the childhood glee is associated with this very hill, that maybe I grew up here, that maybe I played as a child here. Forcing the feeling, trying to bring memories out does no good and the feeling dies, leaving me with a hollow heavy-gut sensation of loss. Thankfully, my lodgings are down hill. I doubt I would have the will to climb. Fortunately, gravity will assist my journey back to the room and the journal that resides there, awaiting my return.

Before I reach the spot where the church stands, I pause to look at two shops that jut out from the hill. They've been built on a platform that defies the slope and results in a wall, the top of which runs horizontal and creates a wedge of brick that is two foot high at one end and thirty-foot tall at the other. It has a strange sense of familiarity. At the tall corner, the returning wall does not form a right angle; what is it obtuse? Acute? Whatever, it is less than ninety degrees. Because of the angle, the corners of the bricks jut out by just under an inch. A sensation comes to my mind that feels like memory and prickles the hairs on my neck. Instinctively, I reach just above head height with my right hand and place my fingertips on the sliver of jutting brick. I lift my left foot and place the toe of my shoe on a brick wedge around the corner, and push. Before I realise what's occurring, I'm ten-foot above the pavement, free climbing the toe and finger holds on the corner of the wall. I scramble down, quickly, when the headlights of an ascending car falls onto the wall and casts from me a hard shadow. I climbed this wall as a child, I just know it; I feel it.

I glance at the church as I pass, certain that it must contain some sort of similar memory; it fails to deliver. Similarly, the recreation ground where I perhaps played as a child offers no supporting evidence. Arriving at the main road that runs parallel to the railway line, I take in an old building that's accessed by crossing a road bridge that spans the tracks: a junior school called Brightside: it looks anything but. Did I go there? I wonder. At the very bottom of the hill flows a river that runs black with nighttime reflection. It seems so familiar, all of it, and yet it also seems so alien. Thrusting cold hands into my trouser pockets and hunching my shoulders against the cold, I turn to the left and set out in the direction of The Foundry.

The pub in the near distance is a welcome sight. Standing alone on the railway side of the road, the darkness surrounding it makes the glow of its windows all the more inviting. I'm about to cross the road earlier than strictly necessary to take a glance over the wall at the railway tracks and the river, when I hear angry sounding voices coming from an a narrow passageway on my side of the road, around fifteen paces away. A fairly wide passage, it cuts between the rear gardens of the terraced houses that front the road opposite the pub, and the rear walls of the industrial units to my left. The passage is poorly lit. Anyone walking through there is surely asking for trouble and it sounds like someone found it.

My heart pumps a fast beat as I approach with caution and peer around the wall. Three youths – two tall and well built, one blond the other ginger, the third shorter and quite fat – are gathered around an older looking man who brandishes a stick, shaking it at them, its shiny bulbous end catching what little light there is in the alley. "Clear off," he snarls. "Afoor I split yer skull."

"Don't be daft, old man," one of the taller youths says, his voice a mix of anger and amusement, as he steps away from the slow swing of the old guy's stick. "Just hand over the wallet."

"Never," he snaps, swinging through a half circle to face the other two. "Clear off. Bloody hoodlums."

Fuck. I recognise the walking stick before I recognise the man. It's Arthur. He'll be on his way to The Foundry for his nightly beer, with his note-crammed wallet. *I could do without this. I could really do without this.* Twisting out of sight, I lean my back against the wall and think of walking back down the road a distance before crossing to the other side and making my way to the pub. He should just give them the wallet; then it'd be done with. He should call it a lesson: leave the cash at home or in the bank and come out with only what you need for the night; don't take short cuts down dark alleyways. If he gives them the wallet, they'll likely just run off and leave him be. I won't have to get involved then.

If I have to wade in there, I'm likely to get my head kicked in.

There's three of them and only one of me.

A quick glance reaffirms my impression that Arthur has no intention of handing over his wallet. He thrusts his stick forward, ramming its club-like end into the fat lad's chest. The lad staggers back a couple of paces, his flesh wobbling like a jelly.

With a grunt, Jelly Boy growls, "fucken old git," steps forward, snatches the stick, and throws it with a clatter to the ground.

Give Arthur his due, he doesn't back down. Instead he raises his fists, old bareknuckle style, like a fairground boxer from days of old: elbows tucked in, fists at chin height, the backs of his hands facing his opponents and ready to pop a gentlemanly punch. One of the taller youths mirrors Arthur's stance, circling back and forth, ducking from Arthur's slow punches and laughing cruelly as they miss by a mile.

"I've had enough of this," Jelly Boy complains, and pushes Arthur to the ground. "Hand the wallet over now, afore I kick yer ribs in."

Arthur grips the front of his coat, holding it shut. He's got no intention of giving up that wallet, no matter what they throw at him.

Bloody hell.

I step into the alley, adrenaline pumping me with nervous energy. They don't notice me, even though I'm standing in plain sight. "Leave him alone." The squeak in the final word gives away the fact that I'm bricking it. Hopefully, they'll just move along now that there's a witness to their cowardice.

"Whoa! It's fucken Jack Reacher." Ginger reels back with an emphasised show of theatrical fear, causing the other two to laugh.

"Keep movin' if yer know what's good fer yer," Jelly Boy advises, before hawking a capture of phlegm and spitting on the ground, marking half the distance between us.

"Right. And let you give this old fella a kicking." My arms are trembling, my legs too, but I just about manage to prevent it from entering my voice. I'm not exactly frail looking, and if I act brave they might think twice about taking me on.

"If he just hands over the wallet," snarls Blondie, leaning into Arthur's face, "and stops being such an old dick, nobody's gonna get hurt. Worrabout it old un, you wanna hand it over now, save us from havin' to sort out Mr Reacher?"

So much for my hope that they'll simply move along; they're acting as if I'm not even here.

Blondie reaches down, trying to get his hand inside Arthur's coat. Most likely because of my presence,

Arthur looks even less likely than ever to give up his wallet. "Bloody hoodlums," he growls, and wraps both arms over his front.

I take a step forward, arms slightly to the side, chest puffed up to try and look intimidating, hoping the leather coat adds to the effect, not really knowing what I'm going to do if they decide to take me on. Hopefully they're also putting on a show. Ginger and Jelly Boy step forward, matching the amount by which I've closed the distance so that we're each only a foot away from being toe-to-toe on Jelly Boy's phlegm.

Blondie gives Arthur a backhanded slap on the cheek. "Just give it up, you old goat," he growls.

Time to put up or shut up, I reckon, and I take a quick step forward. Ginger swings a wild left hook towards my face, and seemingly of its own volition my right forearm sweeps it aside. Jelly Boy rushes into my left, as Ginger throws a jab with his right. I smash my left elbow into the mush of Jelly Boy's face and use the momentum to lean right. Ginger's straight jab brushes my shoulder as I continue to twist away from him.

Jelly Boy is on the deck, both hands to his face, his nose gushing with blood. "Fucker's broke me nose." He groans, as Ginger loses his balance and collides with him, clashing his knee into Jelly Boy's head.

Blondie jumps to his feet, and approaches me with his chin thrust forward, knees slightly bent, feet apart, clenched fists held out from his body at hip height. He looks menacing, like he can handle himself better than the other two. Ginger steadies his near fall by bouncing back from the wall to the rear of Jelly Boy. Without pause he's heading back for another go. He's a little more cautious now though, swinging from side to side and edging to my left so that he's on the exact opposite side of me to Blondie.

They rush me together. Surprising myself, I twist on the spot, turning clockwise, swinging my left foot into a high arc that smashes into Ginger's jaw. In one fluid motion, I swipe a scything right hand into Blondie's throat. Glancing quickly to my rear, I see Ginger crashing into the wall, his hands taking most of the impact. Blondie reaches for his throat with his right hand. He's gasping for breath. He makes a pathetic attempt at punching me with his left: wild swings that go nowhere near to hitting their mark.

Ginger's regained his balance, and looks ready to rush me again. Without a second thought, I swing my foot, hard, as if trying to send a football the entire length of the pitch, and strike into Blondie's groin. He slumps straight to his knees, gasping, and rolls onto his side where he empties his guts. Turning to face Ginger, I skip from foot to foot, my hands rolling loose before my face, ready to strike when he's close enough. I'm finding it hard to believe what I've just done. My mind is racing, but I adopt an expression of pure calm, and arrogantly beckon Ginger forward with a curl of my finger.

"Fuck this," he mutters, casting a look to the ground where both of his thuggish associates are groaning and gasping for air. Ginger then turns heel and takes off, running along the main road in the opposite direction from the pub.

For a moment, I consider going after him. He's got off light compared to his mates, but beating them up wasn't the objective; heck, I didn't even know I was capable of doing such a thing.

"You alright, Arthur?"

"Just a bruised pride," he answers, as I help him to his feet and hand him his stick. "Take me to The Foundry, will ya. I need a drink. We'll phone the coppers from there."

I couldn't have walked away, I couldn't have left Arthur to take a kicking, but getting the police involved is the last thing I need.

CHAPTER

16

I close the black notebook with a snap of satisfaction, having just written about my surprising fighting ability. It may be common knowledge to my other self, but there's been no mention of it in the journal, so far. Having said that I've just read a further twenty pages and I haven't managed to take in a single word of it. My mind keeps wandering to the folks in the bar downstairs and wondering if they will stick to their promise to keep me out of it when the police arrive.

A knock on the door flips my stomach into my throat, and closing the journal, I sit tight and quiet.

"Hey," a female voice says. "You're safe now. The cops have gone."

"Okay." I blow a sigh of relief. "Thanks."

"People down in the bar wanting to buy you a drink."

Opening the door a fraction, I take a glance towards the stairs before opening it a little wider and stepping back as an invitation for Nicky to enter the room. She steps in, eases the door to a close, and then leans against the frame. Her cheeks look a little flushed, and she's breathing rather heavily through flared nostrils. Looking me in the eye, Nicky runs a slick of moisture over her plump upper lip and then twists her mouth into shape that's somewhere between a smirk and a pout.

"Sounds like you were quite the hero, from what Arthur's told the police."

Nicky subtly gyrates her hips, as she reaches up towards her ear and twists a strand of hair around her finger.

"Naw." I shake my head, and avert my eyes from the sultry look that Nicky's casting. "I just did what anyone would've done."

"I doubt that. Arthur reckons you were like Bruce Lee. Karate kicks, and chops, an' all, he says. Coppers reckon they've a fair idea who attacked him from the description, and Arthur says there'll be no room for doubt cause they'll be black and blue with one of 'em hardly able to stand up straight. Crown jewels crushed, he said." Her mouth bunches and then forms a smirk, and then she lets out a breathy-chuckle.

"What did he tell them about me?"

"He didn't tell them you were staying here, if that's what you mean. Said he'd never seen you before; that you just showed up. Said you chased after the Ginger-haired one, and that he made his way here on his own."

"And they believed him?"

Nicky shrugs and takes a step away from the door, a step closer to me, her chest rising and falling in time with the long and slow and deep intakes of breath. "Seemed to."

"And nobody else told?"

"Nope. Thing is, though, what I'm wondering is, why the big secret?"

Nicky steps to within a foot of me and leans forward slightly, placing her palm against my chest. I can feel the tremulous air escaping her nostrils as she looks up into my eyes, her fingers flexing against my pectoral muscle. Her lips part ever so slightly before she gently draws the lower lip between her teeth. She places her free hand onto my shoulder and draws herself closer still.

I swallow as she elevates her height and moves in for what I anticipate will be an extremely passionate kiss.

I almost dive in, almost succumb; I'm most definitely aroused. At the last moment, our lips almost touching, I take a step back. "I'm sorry, Nicky, but I have a girlfriend. More than that, really… we live together."

Nicky shrugs her shoulders with a style bordering

on comedic, and throws me a warm smile that forms cute dimples in her cheeks. Her eyes sparkle in the half-light cast by the bedside lamp. She looks pleased rather than disappointed. "Figures, I guess. Why wouldn't someone like you already be taken?"

"I wouldn't want to take advantage–"

Nicky shakes her head, her smirk growing all the wider. "You do know you're making it all the harder for me to walk away. You could have... I'd already scored you high, and now you've gone up a couple more notches. Anything else, and you're going to blow through the top of my scale."

I shake my head and form what I hope is a humble expression. "Really, you don't know me."

"I don't, do I? But I can tell you're one of the good guys. A regular Lone Ranger."

"Yeh, right."

"I mean it. She's a lucky girl…"

"Penny. Penelope." I wonder if she genuinely considers herself lucky. "I think I'm the lucky one, truth be told. Like I say, you don't know me."

Nicky probes her cheek with her tongue. "So, why not tell me? I can keep a secret; what's yours?"

"No secret, Nicky. I just don't want the police to know it was… The fighting… Even though I was helping Arthur…" I'm stalling somewhat, struggling to come up with something that will satisfy her curiosity enough to allow her to let it drop. Nothing's coming to mind, until… "Some things just stick to you is all. Got done for ABH a few years back. It was self-defence, but I went a bit far, hurt the guys that attacked me. Got a suspended sentence, and if this…"

"Grievous bodily harm is the worse one though, isn't it, not actual?"

I'm uncertain, having made the entire thing up, but I nod in reply to Nicky's question all the same.

"Fair enough." Nicky's nodding; she's bought it. "I can see why you wouldn't…"

I grimace a look of genuine guilt, not for the ABH but for lying to a decent girl. Nicky mirrors the grimace.

"I don't think it'd have gone against you. Arthur put you in a real good light. But I can understand you not wanting to risk it."

"I went a bit over the top. I was angry, you know. Feel a bit bad about it, to be honest."

Nicky shrugs the serious air from her shoulders and skips to the door with a Disney-like bounce in her step. "You'll likely feel a bit less guilty when you see Arthur's shiner. So, come on, get your cute arse downstairs and gracefully accept the old guy's thanks."

CHAPTER

1 7

My head is pounding from all of the beer I consumed last night, and not yet feeling ready to face breakfast, I open the journal and try to focus on the information it contains. I still have no recollection of writing this stuff, or of the woman who encouraged me to write it. Wondering if I ever will and feeling afraid that this instance, this year, might be the time that I don't even return I feel a hollow weight of despair in my chest, a sensation of deep-seated loss. The alcohol may be playing a part, but I feel physically and emotionally drained. I almost close the journal, intending to stay in the bed and sleep, a large part of me wishing that I could close my eyes and never open them again. A look at the photograph of Penny gives me the boost I need, though, and I dive into the pages once more.

* * *

3rd March 2015

I've already mentioned that I met Penny on the night of her twenty-first birthday, when I was doing a gig. I asked her to come and see me the following week at the same venue. Much to my surprise, she turned up. We've been a couple from then, seeing each other most days, except when she worked nights at the hospital (something she seemed to do more regularly than others).

A few weeks after first meeting Penny, I discovered that she used to live with her grandmother, but that the old lady had died in the previous March, only six months before Penny and I met. Her parents had both died years earlier than that: her mother when Penny was fifteen, and her father when she was ten. That night I discussed it with Pauline. Turns out that Penny's grandmother was one of Pauline's associates (no surprise there. Pauline seems to know everything and everyone within a twenty-mile radius).

Pauline was quite insistent that I look after Penny, and that I not mess her about. She went on to say that Penny had already had too much sadness in her life as it was. That went without saying, as far as I was concerned, but I got the feeling that Pauline meant something more than the fact of her parents dying while she was young. Pauline wouldn't elaborate further, other than to say, "You are not the only one who has repressed memories". She clammed up then, with an obvious look of horror in her eyes that showed how much she regretted opening her mouth.

"And don't take advantage of her," Pauline quickly added.

I had no intention of doing so, and even when I found out how much money she had, I still didn't. To this day I still haven't. Even if I'd been inclined, Pauline would have made my life a misery. Back then, at the beginning, I allowed Penny the ease of thinking I didn't know her secret financial security. I asked little about her life before I came into it, and she offered little voluntarily. That suited me, as it made it all the easier to keep the secret of my missing twenty years.

Penny knows about the missing years now, of course, otherwise I wouldn't be writing it in here. It came out during an argument, last May. I thought she'd have gone mad, but she took it well. My rehearsed protestations of always intending to tell her, but of being afraid of losing her, were not needed.

She said things made more sense, and that she was going to do some research on memory loss. It's a result of that research that Penny suggested this journal. She discovered something called psychogenic amnesia, which I'm not even going to try and explain (Google it). I was twenty-seven at the time: two months away from being twenty-eight. Since I'd woken in London that day, eight years had passed by. In all those years, I'd told nobody other than Pauline about not being able to recall anything of my past.

So, the argument! I'm hoping this will be as useful as the nicer stuff for invoking memory.

It was the first time I'd sung my version of George Ezra's 'Barcelona' live. I can't quite push my voice to the same level of bass as him so I had to make it my own. I'd practised and practised until I was sick of hearing it myself. I assumed Penny would be sick of hearing it too, but I was wrong. When we got back to her flat that night she flung her arms around me and dived in for the longest lasting snog ever. After gaining her breath, she told me how much she loved to hear me sing that song, admitting that it gave her goose-bump-tingles everywhere, winking, and saying, "and I mean, everywhere! And, because of that song, I want you to take me to Barcelona for my twenty-fifth".

I'm sure I don't need to explain the oh-shit feeling. No identity means no passport, if you haven't already gathered that nugget of info, and no passport meant no going to Barcelona. Going abroad was already a bit of a sore subject, because Penny once booked a holiday for both of us in Lanzarote as a surprise to celebrate her graduating as a staff-nurse. We'd been together for just over eighteen months, and although she wasn't happy about me not having a passport, and more so about my refusal to travel into London to get a last minute one, she forgave me. Back then I lied about having commitments, claiming that she'd not given me enough notice and that I didn't want to let my elderly clients down. Truthfully, they do rely on me for more than gardening, but it wouldn't have really been a problem. I suggested that she invite Kaitlyn to go in my place. Secretly I was sick to my stomach that I couldn't go myself. Penny did agree to take Kaitlyn, but made me promise to keep the fact that she had paid for the entire holiday to myself. So on top of not being able to go, I had to pretend that I had paid for it, and refuse Kaitlyn's offer of reimbursement. I also had to question Penny about how she could afford it, because I'd already been pretending that I didn't know about all the wealth she had stashed away. I should have been an actor. Maybe Penny should be too, because she very convincingly made up a story about her grandmother leaving her a little in her will.

Penny came back from that holiday and immediately asked me to move into her flat, stating that she'd missed me every minute of every day she'd been away. I felt it was a bit soon, but she insisted, and it sure beat Pauline's box room. That was two and a half years back, three and a half if you're reading this a year from now. I had some concerns other than the time we'd known each other, and so did Pauline; it's hard to keep big secrets from someone when you live together, she told me. I shelved those concerns, though, and in November of 2012 I left Pauline's spare room and moved in with Penny.

Anyway, the Lanzarote situation fuelled the argument about going to Barcelona, because Penny already had the passport form, and had filled in what she could of it. She presented it to me stating that there was no excuse, she'd allowed plenty of time, and all that I needed were a couple of photographs.

My claimed fear of flying didn't wash. She'd already anticipated it and had booked me onto a course that talked through such fears and claimed a high success rate. My argument of just not being interested in travelling caused a row that lasted a week, and resulted in Penny thinking that I just didn't want to be with her, that for me this relationship was just a casual thing. She wanted to know why I was holding back, what my problem was. Casual thing. It most certainly wasn't, isn't, and seeing her so cut up about it made it all the more difficult for me to keep up the face of indifference that I'd decided to adopt.

One evening, while we were both not really enjoying a favourite film that we were watching, Penny turned to me and asked if I wanted to finish with her. That was the last thing I wanted. I ached to tell her the real reason that I was refusing to go abroad.

And then I did tell her. Everything. I told her about waking up in a doorway in London, about travelling the tube all day, about getting the train to Brookwood, about living in Mrs Gaskell's shed for a few weeks.

I'm going to stop writing now.

I need to talk to Penny about something that happened in those first couple of weeks, when I was living in Pauline's shed. I didn't tell her everything, and looking at these words written on the page has made me feel guilty. I don't want her finding out by reading it in here.

CHAPTER

1 8

10th March 2015.

I left it a while before telling Penny the missing information. Now that she knows, I can write it in here.

One night while I was using Pauline's shed for a place to sleep, I prevented a girl from getting raped on the lane that runs by Mrs Gaskell's property.

When I told Penny, she put a hand to her mouth, and gazed at me through wide eyes. "That was you," she eventually said, patting her chest. With tears rolling down her cheeks, she managed to gasp. "It was me; I was the girl."

Penny had looked familiar on the night of her twenty-first, and now I know why. Fate, it would seem, brought us together.

Penny hasn't let up for over a week now, off

and on, wanting more information from me about the night that she was almost raped. She wants to know how it looked from my perspective. Do I think it was partially her fault? When she bloody well reads it in here she might actually stop asking me, and believe that it was in no way whatsoever her fault.

In case you didn't get that Penny, go back and re-read the prior paragraph. Read it as many times as it takes for it to sink in and be believed. Maybe you were foolish to wander down a deserted lane, alone, in the dark, but no more foolish than any man who does similar and ends up getting mugged.

IT WAS NOT YOUR FAULT!

Assurance is not all that Penny wants, though; she also wants details. She wants to know what happened after. The truth is, I don't remember. I recall quite clearly climbing over the fence, and I recall quite clearly seeing the young woman I now know was Penny on the ground. The man had managed to unfasten her belt, and he punched her on the side of her head when she struggled. She went still at that point, the fight gone from her, and quietly pleaded for him to stop. I recall quite clearly that the man must have heard me approaching, or maybe he sensed it, because he didn't turn around. He suddenly went rigid, like a rabbit caught in headlights. He stopped tugging at Penny's jeans, jumped to his feet and just took off down the lane. I sprinted after him, expecting him to run over the bridge towards the railway station and the large cemetery beyond. That's where I'd have gone if I'd wanted to lose someone.

My legs were cold and stiff. If I'd warmed up, I might have easily caught him. Despite that, I battled on, chasing. He turned onto the muddy towpath, and I clearly recall turning on there in pursuit. As we neared the point where the main road to Guildford crosses over the canal he paused a moment. He was likely deciding between taking to the road or continuing along the footpath. His moment of indecision allowed me to gain some ground. I was feeling less stiff and running faster by this point. He must have chosen the footpath, because I remember focussing on chasing him through the dark tunnel, but then it goes all hazy. Beyond us getting close to the tunnel, my mind is blank.

I've not walked on that patch of towpath since. Walking along the side of the canal towards the tunnel makes me feel queasy. I break out in a cold sweat. As I get close to the bridge I feel waves of nausea. I've tried to overcome it, tried to beat it, but I can't. Eventually it gets so bad that I just have to turn around and walk away. It unnerves me, the tunnel, because it reminds me of the black holes in my memory.

It's only over these past few days I've come to know that a body was found in the canal lock nearest to the tunnel the day after Penny was almost raped. His neck had been broken. Penny doesn't know if it was the man who'd attacked her. She was face to the ground and only saw him from the rear as I chased him down the lane. I was living in Pauline's shed at the time. I had no interest in local news. I was more interested in getting fed and keeping warm to be bothered with anything else. Penny tells me that the photograph in the newspaper didn't look like a rapist, but then what does a rapist look like?

She now wants to know if I killed the man that attacked her.

She claims it won't alter the way she feels about me.

Penny may believe that her feelings won't alter, but I don't.

The truth is, I don't know if I killed the man.

The truth is, I hope I didn't.

The truth is, I'm now keener than ever to know about my past. I'm also more nervous than ever about finding out that it might contain something bad.

The truth is, I'm afraid of losing the best thing in my life.

11th March

Last night I had the most horrific nightmare.

It began with Penny's near rape. Everything unfolded as I remember it, up to the point where I'm chasing the man down the lane and onto the towpath. I'm then running through freezing fog, my icy breath swirling into the frigid cloud. In my nightmarish vision, it eddies around me like an overzealous storm cloud. The fog clears, and I'm on the towpath, running for all I'm worth, but the path is no longer flat, it's steep. It's a steep hill, and I'm running down it. I keep on losing my footing, my feet slipping on the ice-slushed mud, and I get the feeling that I might lurch forward at any moment and tumble into the canal at the side. In this nightmare the canal has become a raging torrent, a fast flowing river that roars by the side of me, splashing painful droplets of ice onto my hot cheeks.

In a shift of perspective, I realise I'm not the one doing the chasing. I'm the one being chased. At the far side of the canal I see two shops that are set back from a tall wall that juts from the hill at a seemingly impossible angle. There's a monkey climbing the corner of the wall. The man chasing is gaining on me. I hear his feet pounding as I glance at a church with a giant dartboard for a door. He's closer now, almost upon me. He grabs my shoulder and spins me around. Momentarily I'm on the roundabout in a child's recreation ground. Unoccupied swings come in and out of my vision, their chains clanking as they tip and fall as if invisible occupants have leapt from them at the peak of their rise.

The canal come river swamps the towpath, and the man grabs hold of my shoulders. Freezing black water rages around our legs.

Standing up is becoming a struggle. He's shaking me violently and calling me a filthy rapist. I argue back, grabbing his shoulders, arguing that he is the rapist. YOU! NOT ME, I yell at the top of my voice. Round and around we turn, until I forget if I was the one being chased or he was. In a surge of strength, I wrestle myself free and trap his head between my arm and my chest. He struggles to get free. The water is rising higher, and flowing faster down the hill that is steadily getting steeper. Using my free hand to push against his forehead, I twist his skull in the same direction by pushing my elbow forward. A sickening crack emanates from his neck. I feel bile rising in my throat as he goes limp, but rather than being heavier, he's lighter. I look at the crook of my arm, and see not the face of a man, but the face of a girl, a young girl, looking up at me with eyes that are dead and lifeless, her feet dangling a foot from the ground. "No," I scream, "No, no, no," as the water rises higher still, drags me from my feet and washes me away past a line of black cars decorated with silver frost, and drags me towards a foggy void.

Penny reckons that the dream means nothing, that it's my worst fears haunting me during sleep. I saw doubt in her eyes, but she claims she has none. I've asked her many times today, but she assures me that she believes me. She's certain I didn't kill that man. I wish I were so certain.

I'm guessing that the nightmare will do nothing to help restore my memories, that it will mean nothing to you/me when reading this a year from now. I don't even know why I wrote it down. I just felt as if I had to.

C H A P T E R

1 9

I've read all of the entries made in March, and April, and May. There is no longer much mention of past events, and the journal is now reading as just that: a record of happenings on the day of writing that I supposedly felt were worth mentioning. Of all those entries, the one that particularly sticks in my mind is the nightmare. Elements of it sound like this place: the shops that jut out of the hill in defiance of the steep angle; the church (although I haven't a clue what the giant dartboard-door might possibly represent); the children's recreation ground. Most haunting though is the idea of chasing the rapist along the towpath and the switching of places. I'm unnerved by the revelation that the man found in the canal had a broken neck. I know I can fight, the events of last night proved that. And then the dead man turned into a girl. What could that possibly mean?

Did I kill a little girl?

Picking up the black notebook, I flick to the pages where I've outlined my fighting ability. I'm going to rip them out, burn them in the sink. *It's incriminating evidence*, I argue to the side of my brain that's telling me not to rip out the pages. Eventually I toss the book onto the bed, still intact. *I'm here to discover the truth,* I decide, *for better or for worse.*

I need to get out for a bit, stretch my legs and get something to eat. I'm sick of reading the journal, and somehow, I don't think it's going to help.

* * *

The shopping mall that I now know as Meadowhall has a plethora of choice when it comes to dining. Given that choice, I plumped for a burger, a very nice burger, a freshly hand-made burger, but all the same, what does that say about me? Does it say anything about me? Given that I have a past history that amounts to only a few days, am I actually modelling the person I am going to be, based on the choices I make? Or, am I unknowingly following a path of choice that is already established in the blank-to-me sections of my mind. Am I like a marble trundling along a well-worn trench?

The nightmare haunted me while I ate.

The nightmare haunted me as I bought a change of clothes.

It played through my head as I changed from the suit to jeans and jumper in the toilet cubical.

The nightmare haunted me while I drank an

overpriced cup of tea in a Costa that was situated in the rear of W H Smiths, and looked out through its window at the hill where I first arrived.

The nightmare is haunting me now, as I sit in the car on a side road that separates the recreational park from the church. Perhaps haunt is not quite the right word: torment is probably more accurate, or niggles.

The nightmare is tormenting me.

The nightmare is niggling me.

Earlier I was thinking that the journal was not going to help, but now I can't help but feel that there is an element of memory in there, that a memory of my past was trying to push its way through the confines of that horrid dream. I continue to stare at the church door, willing for something to come to mind that is worthy of writing in the black notebook that currently rests on the passenger seat. As the most obscure element, the image of a giant dartboard in place of a church door has become an obsession of which I simply can't let go. It flashes in my mind like a giant neon sign that shouts, CLUE!

Through scrappy bushes to the right, I can see the cinder pitch. Two young boys, one at either end, kick a ball back and forth, and I wonder if I have played on there as a child. I have a strong but unfounded belief that I may have grown up here, on this very hill. I was surely the monkey climbing the wall.

That belief means nothing, but I make a note of it in the book anyway.

The church stands within yards of the main road that drops as steeply as the torrent driven river of the nightmare depicted in the journal. To the rear of the church is a large expanse of grassed lawn onto which the large double doors open. Cherry trees, bare of leaf and blossom at this time of year, edge the grass close to the church. Along the length of the lawn, on the side opposite to the spot where I'm parked, a mass of rhododendron bushes have grown into a gigantic tangle that covers a steep banking, around fifteen feet in height. I imagine it would make a wonderful setting for wedding photographs at the right time of year. The edge of the lawn closest to the side road is completely open, giving the lawn the appearance of being a stage.

An image comes to my mind of cycling on the cinder pitch, of turning the handlebars, of leaning to the side, foot down while applying brakes, and skidding scar-like rings into the surface. The park attendant runs along the path leading to the pitch, yelling at me and two others, barking at us to clear off and to stop ruining the all-weather-pitch. People attending a wedding over the road are craning their necks to look over the scrappy shrubs at the commotion. The park keeper chases us out of the upper gate, the exit from the rec, and we cycle onto the road where I'm parked in the car, laughing and taunting the keeper, who's nowhere even near close to catching us. We cycle towards the three foot high banking to the church lawn, building speed as we approach, no consideration for the crowd gathered there taking photographs and waiting to have their moment in the record of the happy couple's day as our bikes take to the air. We cycle fast across the grass, weaving in and out of children and old folks, laughing with delight as the vicar takes the bait and chases us down the street, his robes flapping behind him like the broken wings of an oversized gull.

This feels so much like memory that it surely must be, and although I feel a pang of guilt at the behaviour, I'm also slightly amused.

Is it memory, or is it invention? My mind aches with the battle of trying to decide one way or the other; the concept feels somewhat like trying to rationalise the idea of an infinite universe. There's just nothing concrete to grab a hold of.

I reach for the notebook, intending to scribble down every detail before any of it has a chance to escape. As pen touches paper, another memory hits the picture screen of my mind. I'm on the grass leading up to the church door, there's a young lad with me. The day looks glorious with a clear blue sky and delicate wisps of white cloud. The rhododendron bushes and cherry trees are in full bloom, which would make it spring. Leaning against the bushes is a paper-spiral dartboard that looks fit to break into scraps. Something tells me we found it, or rescued it from a bin or a skip. We're taking turns at playing the game. We're laughing and teasing each other.

The memory shifts.

The dartboard is now flat on the ground on the end of the lawn furthest from the church door. We're standing at the centre of the lawn, launching the darts high into the air, watching as they reach the peak of their climb. They arc and then descend towards the board. We cheer if we get a hit, boo and tease one another for a miss.

Again the memory shifts.

We're standing on the grass at the end furthest away from the church door. The board has unravelled, and is now a paper spiral among the scattered confetti and cherry blossom. The lad I'm with brings his arm back like a javelin thrower and launches his dart with as much might as he can muster. We watch with awestruck delight as it flies towards the church door, but groan as it pierces the grassy ground some twenty feet short of the door. *Closer* he says to me, and I nod with enthusiasm. He retrieves the short-fallen arrow, and we decide on a spot that's not quite at the halfway mark, some forty feet closer than before. I launch one of my three darts. It flies straight and true, hardly dipping as it heads for the church door and strikes home with a satisfying knock. My playmate launches another of his darts. It strikes the door close to mine and emits the same satisfying knock as it buries deep into the heavy timber. *Together,* he says, and we do just that. The two darts strike the door within a split second of each other: knock, knock, to which we cheer. With unspoken agreement, looking at the glee on each other's face, we draw back to throw the final dart that we each hold.

My arm is already nearing the end of the launch. I've thrown this one harder than the previous two, so hard that I feel the ache of the effort in my muscles and joints, the intention being to bury the dart as deep in the wood as it's possible for it to go. The words *deepest in the door wins* are forming in my mind, as my fingers release the dart.

And then I notice that the door is opening.

All thoughts of competition escape my mind and the word *crap* pushes through as the vicar's head appears in the growing gap, a puzzled look on his face to see nobody standing there. The puzzled look instantly morphs into annoyance as he focuses on us, and then explodes into one of alarm as the fast flying darts thwack, thwack, into the door on either side of his head.

Run, we both cry, as the angry gull chases us down the street.

Again the memory shifts.

I'm perched high in a tree along with my dart throwing companion. The tree is situated in the back yard of a house, over the roof of which can be seen the church spire. The vicar exits the rear door of the house, closely followed by a man who looks to be in his mid-twenties. *Martin, I'll bloody kill you when you come down,* he yells. *These were my best bleedin' darts.*

In a shift of perspective, we're now in Martin's kitchen. I'm looking out of the window up at the tall tree that blocks most of the sunlight from entering the room. I'm looking out there, rather than look at the decrepit woman that's sitting in a chair in the corner of the dark room, her flesh so sunken that she looks like a skeleton. She sits and stares and she sucks on her naked gums.

A terrible stench invades my nostrils, as Martin raids the biscuit barrel.

MUM! Martin shouts, as he turns the doorknob of the back door, handing me the unopened packet of custard creams. *Gran's shit in her chair, again.* And then we're walking up the road, sharing the biscuits, laughing, sharing made-up tales, and highlighting the fact that we never want to get so old that we can't get out of a chair when we want to take a dump.

I've filled twelve pages of the notebook with fast-written scrawl. Nothing more comes to mind. I read back over the words I've scribbled, several times. It must be memory; it links to stuff written in the journal: the shops, and the church, and the recreation ground. For those things to enter the same nightmare, I must have been here before. It seems I was a bit of a rogue when I was a lad, but it also seems that I was happy. If it is true, that is, if the memory is true.

CHAPTER

2 0

When I enter The Foundry, I'm greeted by the sound of an electric guitar's acoustic whine as it's plugged into an amp. Nicky spots me, throws me a quick wave, and then skips from behind the bar to meet me halfway.

"Live music, tonight," she says, clapping with girlish glee.

"Just the one guy, or a band?" I tip my head in the direction of the stocky bald-headed guy who's currently tuning the guitar, his long and frizzy ginger beard splayed across a tee-shirt that looks like it might be a piece of concert memorabilia.

Nicky lets out a little chuckle. "Just Z-Crop. There'd be no room for customers in here if we had a full band.

Seemingly satisfied that the guitar is in tune (which it isn't, quite), Z-Crop, rips a riff from the strings and growls, "she's got legs…" The remnants of the riff buzz in the amp as he places the electric guitar onto the stand and takes an acoustic from its case.

"He any good?"

"Yeh, he's okay. He plays here once a fortnight, and the punters seem to like it. Place is usually buzzing. Harry reckons the profit we make on these nights carries us through the rest of the week. Another guy plays the alternate weeks, but the stuff he sings brings in the older crowd. They tend not to spend so much on drinks, but they are better tippers."

I nod my understanding, picturing in my mind how much better it might sound if the guitar was properly in tune, but thinking that Z-Crop likely won't appreciate the input, I decide to keep quiet.

"So, why's he called Z-Crop?"

"Trevor," Nicky hollers, "my friend here wants to know, why Z-Crop?"

Trevor flashes a big grin and pulls his shaggy beard to one side to reveal a ZZ-Top emblem on his shirt. "My favourite band," he says, striking his chest with a clenched fist. "There's only one of me, so only one Z. And if you haven't noticed," he says, slapping his bald head, "nature gave me a premature crop."

"So you're a tribute act?" I say with a huff of amusement.

"Nah, not really. I sing ZZs well known songs, but mostly I give the crowd stuff that they like."

"Nice to meet you man." I clap Trevor on the shoulder, and head for the back door to the stairs.

"Starts at eight," Nicky calls out. "You may as well come down, cause you'll hear it from up there anyway. We turn it up to eleven, don't we Trev?"

"We sure do." Trevor grins at Harry, the landlord, shaking his head behind the bar as he wipes and inspects glasses before placing them on a shelf.

"Okay, I'll come down and give you a listen," I say, "So long as you promise to cover some Justin Bieber."

Trevor pulls a face like he's just chewed on a dung beetle. "You're joking, right?"

"Yeh, I'm joking." Laughing my head off at the private joke, I quickly take the stairs to my room. More reading, I think, before taking a shower.

* * *

June 20th 2015.

Long while since I wrote anything in here. Three reasons: I've been busy with the gardening. There hasn't really been anything worth writing about. I honestly didn't think I'd disappear next January, which would make writing this thing a complete waste of time. After today, I'm not so sure about that.

Penny and I are in a village called Castleton, which is in the north of Derbyshire, close to a city called Sheffield. We decided we could do with a break, a change of scenery, and I picked here. Don't know why. Just liked the look and sound of the Peak District National Park, I guess, and Barcelona or anywhere else by plane is still not an option.

Right now, Penny is in the shower. I thought about sneaking in and joining her, but decided to write this instead. I must be bonkers. We're going to go out for a meal and a drink, and boy do I need one. Today was a bit... odd.

There's this cave here that's called Peak Cavern, originally it was called The Devil's Arse. Apparently it's called that because of flatulent noises that come from inside the cave when floodwater is draining away. A cave that farts! Brill. All the caves here are open to the public, and I just thought it'd be great to tell people we went to Derbyshire and explored the Devil's Arse. Pen wasn't all that keen - I think she's a bit claustrophobic - but she agreed to go.

Peak Cavern boasts the largest cave opening in the British Isles, and the walk up to it, hand in hand with Penny, was spectacular. The river Styx flows from the cave and down through the village, and you follow that up to a limestone gorge with 280 foot high vertical cliffs. A castle sits on top of the cliff and to my mind it felt like something from a fantasy film. The cave entrance is hidden from view as you walk up the path, and as we neared the bend, I held my breath in expectation of being overwhelmed.

I was not overwhelmed; I was petrified.

As we rounded the corner and my eyes fell into the gaping black void, an opening that literally swallowed the light of day, Penny complained that I was squeezing her hand too tightly.

My heart started beating so fast I felt that it would shatter my ribs.

My mouth went dry.

My lungs burned as I forgot to breath.

The strength went from my legs and, feeling that I might collapse, I edged my way towards the fence that guarded the steep drop down to the gushing stream below. Once there I slid to the ground, my back against the fence and my head between my knees. I could hear the fear in Penny's voice, as she demanded to know if I was okay. I could hear people crowding around asking the same kind of question, some claiming that I was having a panic attack and that I should be given *room to breathe.*

Eventually my heart rate slowed, saliva returned to my desiccated tongue, and I managed to get my breathing under control.

I don't know what brought it on, but I can honestly say that I have never felt as afraid as I did when looking into the black mouth of that cave. That's not quite true. Trying to approach the tunnel on the canal feels similar.

I don't know if it means anything, but I thought it best to write it down.

Penny's ready now. Signing off :~)

* * *

A quick glance at my watch tells me it's a quarter to seven. I've not yet showered, but if I'm quick, I should have time to get myself downstairs and ask Nicky if she knows where this cave is.

CHAPTER

2 1

Nicky stops polishing the table near to the stairs when I enter the room. She stands for a moment in silence, duster in one hand, tin of polish in the other. I notice the dark green varnish on her nails is perfectly applied. A hesitant smile crosses her face and then almost fades to nothing as she glances at Harry. Shaking her head she resumes polishing the table. Harry is standing behind the bar, leaning on the counter, his face plastered with a glum expression. It's twenty minutes past seven, a glance at the clock opposite the bar tells me, and there are only a handful of people in the place.

"I guess it gets busy closer to eight?"

"It will do," Nicky replies, "but I reckon it'll empty just as quickly. Trevor's had to go. Threw his guts up in the bog, told Harry he felt like crap, and said he had to leave. Didn't even take his stuff. Said he'd be back for it tomorrow, or he'd get his brother to come and get it if he didn't feel well enough."

"Bummer; I was looking forward to it... Erm, might seem an odd question, but have you ever seen the Devil's Arse?"

Nicky throws me a look that's half puzzled bewilderment and half amusement, her mouth twists into the cute smirk I've already come to recognise as the predicator of a wise crack, and she chuckles a little before saying, "I've seen Harry bending to get mixers off the bottom shelf. Does that count?"

"Har, bloody-har," Harry voices with a big measure of derision. "If I weren't so pissed off, I might've actually laughed."

Nicky sniffs and grimaces. "Gonna be fun working here tonight," she mutters.

"Been a quiet week as it is," Harry complains. "Rely on these Saturdays, I do." He looks at me with eyebrows elevated. "Don't suppose you fancy re-enacting your Lone Ranger night, Tom? Folks spent a little more, along with their talk of Enter the Dragon."

"Harry!" Nicky glares at the landlord, still gritting her teeth as he mouths a silent sorry and mimes the pulling of a zip across his tight-lipped mouth.

"If you think Trevor wouldn't mind me using his equipment," I say, somewhat hesitantly, as I approach the bar with Nicky close behind, already regretting opening my mouth but somehow still failing to shut it, "I could... you know... perform."

Harry's eyes open wide and he throws a glance at

Nicky who curls around me, leans on the bar and looks up into my eyes. "You can sing and play guitar?"

"I think so."

"You think so…?" Harry scowls with puzzlement, a hand on his round gut and his index finger inside the shirt, as best as I could tell, fingering his belly button. "Surely, you either can or you can't."

Naturally I don't want to say, *according to a journal that I supposedly wrote, I apparently can play guitar and sing to a proficient level, but that I have no actual memory of having ever done so.* Besides, just because it's written in the journal that doesn't mean it is necessarily true. "What I mean is, I can play and I can sing, but I don't know if I'll be good enough."

It is a way of testing the honesty of the journal, but maybe it's not the best I could have come up with.

"I'll tell you what…" Harry makes his way from behind the bar, sniffing his finger as he heads towards Trevor's equipment. He pats the amp with Z-Crop emblazoned on its side. "If you're even halfway to good, you're on. And if Mr Z isn't happy about you using his equipment, he can bloody well try and sue me, which he won't, not if he ever wants to play here again, which I'm sure he does, because if he had any better options he wouldn't be playing here in the first place." Harry turns on the amp and then, much to my relief, dials it down to two. "Come on then… show us what you've got."

I can feel sweat dribbling down my back. I look at Nicky, who's all cherry-red smile and expectation as she leans on the counter top, her chin in her hands. I'm going to look a right twonk if I can't actually do this. Maybe I did write the journal, maybe I didn't, but if I did, there really is no saying I'm not a fantasist.

Remembering that the guitar is not quite in tune, I decide that tuning will be a good place to start; if I can't do that, I'll gracefully bow out. Drawing in a huge lungful of air and blowing away the tension, I strike the bottom e string and then give the key a slight turn before striking it again. Harry rolls his lower lip, as I continue to repeat the procedure, and turns to look at Nicky with a raised brow.

"Not quite in tune," I tell him, moving up to the b string. "I thought as much earlier, but I didn't think it my place to tell Trevor."

The guitar now fully tuned, feeling a little more confident, I decide to leave out the singing until I've actually confirmed my ability to play a tune. I try to recall music in my mind. I try to imagine notes scribed onto a sheet of paper, but there's nothing. I try to recall a tune as if it's the rehearsed script of a play, and still, nothing comes. This was a big mistake. I glance to the side at Harry, who's glancing at Nicky, who's glancing across the room at the customers – three guys that look to be in their early twenties. The three of them are gazing in my direction no doubt in expectation of hearing a tune, but looking as if they'd be equally as delighted to see someone fall flat on their face as to be entertained.

I'm about to hand the guitar to Harry and say, *sorry mate, I can't do this, nerves got the better of me,* when a riff enters my mind. It uncoils as if being played in the synapses of my brain. It's as if I can actually hear it echoing on the inside of my skull. My fingers flash across the strings, seemingly of their own volition. A striking tune curls from the amp that I instantly know upon hearing it as 'Layla' by Derek and the Dominos.

In my head I'm singing the lyrics. I'm hitting every note on the guitar, I'm recalling every word in the song, but I'm not yet ready to trust my vocal chords to be as cooperative as the strings. Before finishing the tune, my eyes closed, I segue into Aerosmith's 'Angel' – a song that's been on my mind since I first arrived here – lifting the guitar's neck high in the air, bending the strings, I sing the first lines and open my eyes to meet a look of open adoration on the face of Nicky. Filled with instant guilt, I get a strong image of Penny in my mind's eye as I recall singing that song to her on the night of her twenty-first birthday. The journal indicated that when I sang that song to her I meant every single word of it. I now feel the truth of that declaration. A tingle chases the length of my spine and spreads a cold shiver through the hairs on my neck as for the first time she enters my head with the weight of a true memory. The love I feel for her is so powerful that it brings a tear to my eye and momentarily robs me of a voice.

Not wishing to finish the Aerosmith song with Nicky looking on, possibly with the impression that I'm naming her as my angel, and asking for her to save me tonight, I segue into George Ezra's 'Barcelona', knowing that the girl I genuinely long to hold once more is Penny, knowing that I want to sort out these issues associated with my memory so that I can ask her to let me hold her for ever more.

"Turn it up," one of the young guys sitting at the far side of the room shouts, as I merge the tune into Ezra's 'Budapest'.

Harry flicks the amp off, forcing me to sing a cappella for the few moments it takes me to realise.

"Eight o'clock if you want to hear any more." Harry claps me on the shoulder, and then taps his watch as he looks over at the guy who called for the music to be turned up. "And, for once, you'll pay yer tenner like everyone else."

"Was it okay, then?" I ask, pulling the guitar's strap over my head and sitting the instrument on its stand.

"You joking?" Harry shakes his head and plants his fists on the flab hanging over his hips. "Best frigging sound that's ever graced these walls. Beltin' lad. And that's you tuning up? Bloody beltin'."

"That! Was! Amazing!" Nicky emphasises every

word with a snap of her hands. "Wow! You should be playing down the arena, not in here. Wow."

The guy who asked for the music to be turned up is already handing to Harry thirty pounds in payment for himself and his two mates. He tips me a nod of appreciation, and glances at one of his friends, a guy who is on the phone telling someone to get their arse into gear and get down to The Foundry 'cause they're staying put.

"Those guys normally leave ten minutes into Trevor's act," Nicky informs me. "Just in here for a couple of decent, cheap pints to start the night off. You must have impressed 'em to get 'em to hand over their cash and not head off into town."

The pride this information instils is simultaneously tempered with a measure of guilt. My intention was to help Harry out of a fix, not to make Z-Crop look amateurish. I get a strong impression I underestimated my ability when writing the journal, but having said that, putting on a full performance to a bigger more attentive audience may not go quite so well as the practice; there are nerves to consider for one. With that thought, a coil of trepidation squirms through my gut and for a moment I feel a sensation of watery sickness.

"I hope the actual night lives up to their expectations."

Nicky shakes her head, the cute twisting smirk of

amusement crossing her lips. "Humble as well. Don't worry, you're gonna smash it. I'm predicting a busy night."

"I'm predicting the need of a drink."

"Brandy for the nerves?" she mocks, skipping behind the bar singing a few of the more salient lines from 'Angel'.

What have I done, I think, already omitting that song from my mental playlist. I don't want her getting the wrong impression. If it weren't for Penny though... maybe that impression wouldn't be so wrong.

"Whose song is that, anyway?" Nicky places a pint before me, leans against the bar and looks up into my eyes as if I've genuinely burst through the roof of the man-scale she mentioned only yesterday. "I love it."

"It's Aerosmith."

"Oh, I've heard of them. Will you sing it in full, later?"

"Maybe," I say, wishing she hadn't asked, and adding, "it's Penny's favourite song."

A brief look of disappointment crosses Nicky's expression, and I'm left with a sizeable measure of guilt topped with a hint of *what if that journal hadn't been in the glove box?*

* * *

I've been playing for almost two hours with only a

twenty-minute break. The amp is cranked up, and I'm really in the zone. The place is absolutely packed: according to Harry, the fullest it's ever been. Song after song streams into my mind carrying passengers of memory on their lyrical fluidity. I've played a varied set of old-school rock ranging from Derek and the Dominos to Zeppelin to Bon Jovi, I've sung Beatles' and Stones' tracks, and I've sung more modern tunes by George Ezra and Jake Bugg. Everything has been met by rapturous applause, and cheers, and whistles. My confidence has grown a little more with each. Harry has been grinning from ear to ear all night, as both he and Nicky have been kept constantly busy at the bar. My worries and concerns had completely dissolved but, as I glance at the clock and think *this is the last song,* a knot draws in my gut.

This is pretend.

This is an act.

When the last chord is struck, reality resumes, a reality in which I still have no clue who I am or where I came from.

I put the electric guitar to one side and plug in the acoustic.

I have no idea what the last song is going to be, but my fingers seem to know as they trip a fast dance over the strings. *Diddle-a-do, diddle-a-do, dum-do, dum-do,* they strum, over and over, repeating the melody, faster and faster, maintaining a pace I can't quite believe I'm

154

capable of. The place falls to silence as I play, one note overlapping the last creating the impression of more than one instrument. Music echoes around the silent walls. The words come to me mere seconds before they need to be sung, and I instantly know the song to be Fleetwood Mac's 'Big Love'. I feel a heavy psychological pain entering my soul. That pain flies from my throat as a gritty angry growl when I sing about looking for love. It brings a hint of sadness as I sing about a house on a hill. The words genuinely feel as though they have personal meaning to me. The words of the song are surrounded with a blinding darkness, and a sense of longing, and a deep-seated feeling of loss. The words and the feelings spiral through my mind as I go into an instrumental section, music that runs faster and at a higher pitch that reminds me of a woman wailing. My eyes are closed, my head dipped; I open them momentarily to see that my fingers are a blur as they pluck the strings with lightning ferocity. As I begin to sing the next set of words I travel on auto with the guitar playing, and a seemingly separate portion of my mind analyses their relevance. *I really did wake up feeling alone with it all, and I really do wake up only to fall.*

The significance of words that could easily have been written to suit my own circumstance, bring a measure of anger, an anger that colours the tone of my singing. My guitar playing is flawless, but some of the musicality has left my voice. I'm now growling the words, filling them with heartfelt passion and pain and darkness. The anger enters the guitar playing as I strum fast harsh hard chords and, coming towards a climactic close I yell, "Ooo, argh, ooo, argh, OOO, ARGH!"

The room falls deathly silent, save for the buzz of the amp that still carries the fading remnants of the final clashing chord. So quiet is it in here, that I look up and open my eyes and expect to see an empty room. Every occupant of the room shares a silent connection with me, mouths agape, as if stunned, shocked maybe by the closing cries of pure expression.

Too much anger, I'm thinking. *Too crazy? Too passionate?*

I look at Nicky. She shakes her head from side to side, and mouths a silent, *wow.*

The young guy of the three who heard me practicing, the one who decided to stay here rather than venture into town for the usual Saturday night piss-up, claps, slowly, as if coming out of a trance. "Fuckin' brilliant," he shouts, as others join in with the applause.

With no fresh song to interrupt, the applause goes on and on. Someone then shouts "more, more." Others join in the call.

I glance at Harry. He nods, but holds his hand up,

displaying a single digit.

I pluck a few strings and generate soft spiralling notes of lute-like quality. The cheers and calls for more fade as I allow the music to build. As with 'Big Love', I have no idea what the song is, but the muscle memory of my fingers carry the tune long enough for my brain to catch up. I realises as the words enter my mind that it is 'Go Insane', another Fleetwood song. The song's message of losing power in the world where I reside feels particularly redolent, and fills me with sadness as I sing about it driving me insane. My voice gradually colours with anger again. I pick up the tempo with clashing chords, and wonder why the reference to her being a lot like you sits so strong in my thoughts.

* * *

"That really was amazing." Nicky takes a sip of her rum and coke, and places the half-full glass on the table. She slides lower in the large wooden chair, places her bare right foot onto the edge of the seat and hugs her knee. The varnish on her nails, so perfect when the night began, is now chipped at the edges. "You really are a fantastic singer," she says, her voice breathy as she gazes at me with the hot smouldering look she been giving since the place emptied of its last enthusing customer, "and an even better guitarist."

Harry picks up a full pint and downs it without activating his swallow reflex even once. Wiping a hand across the dribbles at the corners of his smiling mouth, he expels a sigh of satisfaction. "Ready for that." Harry places the froth-coated glass onto the table, before leaning close to me, the smell of yeasty beer flavouring his breath. "Consider your bill for the room settled," he says. "I second Nicky's opinion, Tom, and I want you to play here next week. For pay, of course," he adds, as I twist my mouth into a grimace. "Goes without saying."

"I don't know if I'll still be here next week, besides, I don't have my own guitar and amp."

"Bloody hell." Harry scowls and thrusts his jaw forward, showing his lower teeth, like an overweight bulldog.

Nicky chuckles. "You've already told people he'll be playing, haven't you."

"Yeh!" he says, among other partially indecipherable grumbles. "Might've mentioned it to one or two of 'em." He slips his hand into his shirt and swirls a finger into his belly button while he continues to grumble. "Too good for one night only. Won't you change your mind? I'll get Mr Z to let you use his stuff."

"Tell you what. If I'm still here, and if Mr Z doesn't mind, I'll play."

"Fair enough. Another drink?"

"Go on then. Ta."

Harry heads to the bar with both our empty glasses, still grumbling and muttering. He really is a bulldog, I think, as he scratches his expansive behind.

"You reckon you'll still be here then?" Nicky asks, bringing her other leg into the seat and hugging both knees together. She glances at her nails, allows a momentary look of annoyance to wash over her face, and she mouths a silent, *fuck*. As they create the shape of the silent curse, her lips form a sexy pout that draws me in and fills me with warmth.

"Doubt it," I say, burying the sensation, "but you never know."

"I haven't had chance to ask, but what was that earlier about the Devil's Arse?"

"It's a cave, not far away, I think, at a place called Castleton. I just wondered if you knew of it."

Nicky rolls her lower lip and takes a moment to think. "I know Castleton. I know there's a few caves there, but I don't know one called that."

"I think it's also called Peak Cavern."

"Ah! I know that one. Been in it. Big opening, closest to the village."

Harry sets two pints, and a Malibu-and-coke on the table before groaning his weight into the seat "They changed it from Devil's Arse when Queen Victoria visited, so as not to offend her," he says.

"You goin' ter take a look?"

"Thought I might, yes."

"To do with tracking your family history?" Nicky asks. I smell coconut from the drink on her breath and feel a strong sense of recollection that quickly fades to nothing.

Already swallowing a mouthful of beer, I simply nod my reply. "Fancy a run there with me, tomorrow?" I ask, before wiping the beer froth from my top lip. "Show me the way."

"Yeh, if you like," she replies, her face lighting up at the prospect.

CHAPTER

2 2

That's it then, Kaitlyn now knows I was almost raped and that Tom prevented it from actually happening. On a low-ebb, on this lonely Sunday morning, she caught me off guard. To be honest it feels like a load off: a trouble shared, and all that.

"You could have told me," she says, tears welling in her eyes, her expression switching from pity to anger, before she throws her arms around my shoulders and pulls me into a strong hug of comfort.

"It happened before I knew you," I sob back.

Kaitlyn lets go, and we retreat to our respective ends of the sofa.

"I was eighteen. Didn't tell any one, not even Gran. Her ticker was dodgy and I didn't want anything to make it worse; she was all I had. So, I kept quiet about it. And, I didn't actually get raped. Sure, it shook me up. Scared me to tears. Took some getting over. I still think about it now, sometimes. Can't help thinking about what would have happened… you know… if Tom hadn't."

"Well I hope Tom gave your attacker a good kicking."

"Whoever it was, he got away. Tom never managed to catch him."

"Pity." A questioning look of realisation comes to Kaitlyn's face, words on the verge of spilling from her mouth seemingly captured by a scramble of thoughts in her mind. "You never did tell me how Tom manages to drive if he's got no licence. I know he's insured, because he struck that woman's car that time when he was giving me a lift home."

"Yeh!" I don't quite manage to shelve the grimace. "Thought you might have forgotten about that. You have to promise to keep it quiet."

"Sounds ominous." Kaitlyn adjusted her position on the sofa and looks at me with serious intent.

"Promise."

"Alright, I promise."

"Well, you know Tom used to lodge with an elderly woman called Pauline?" Kaitlyn nods, her expression unreadable. "Well, he tended her garden and did other odd jobs. He then started doing the same for friends of hers, but he was carrying his tools in a wheelbarrow, which obviously wasted a lot of time. One day, she told him her grandson's old van was in her garage, and he was welcome to use it. When he told her he felt that he knew how to drive, but he didn't have a licence, she said no problem, and presented him with her grandson's. She made him promise to use it only for things in relation to the car insurance, and he agreed. That's it. Better than driving without insurance, I suppose she was thinking."

Kaitlyn scowls. "Bloody hell, how many more secrets are there? Did Tom tell you that story or did the old lady?"

"Tom told me."

"And have you ever asked her to confirm it? He might have just stolen her grandson's licence and made it up."

"I haven't asked her… But I don't think he'd have made it up."

Kaitlyn shakes her head, a look of worry in her eyes. "There are a lot of things adding up here, Pen. Still he stopped you from being attacked, so I guess I can overlook a bit of minor fraud. I still can't believe that you already knew Tom when we met him at the Pig, and you never said anything."

"Well, I didn't know him, exactly, not really." My hand waves the yes/no gesture.

"But… how could you not, if…? I thought… You just said he stopped you from being raped."

I nod my understanding of her confusion. "I didn't know it was Tom that night in the lane, not until he told me, last March. He ran after the guy, the… Anyway, when he didn't catch him, he came back to the lane, but I'd already scarpered. Ran to Gran's as quick as my legs would carry me. We were discussing about how he couldn't remember his past. Tom was saying how miserable it often made him feel, how most of the time he puts a brave face on, and I told him I wish I could forget some of my past. I broke into tears and it all came out. He knew it was me that night in the lane, but I didn't know it was him."

"But surely you knew his face, from when he stopped the guy from…?"

"No. It was dark. It all happened so fast. Didn't see Tom's face, and I didn't see the other guy's either."

Kaitlyn blows out a lungful of tension and rakes her fingers through her hair. "Bloody hell, Pen. How'd you know it wasn't Tom?"

"What d'you mean?"

"If you didn't see the face of the man who tried to rape you, and you didn't see the face of the man who came to your rescue, what's to say that the would-be-rapist wasn't Tom? What's to say that the other man wasn't your rescuer?"

"Tom's the one that was living in Pauline's shed."

"What does that prove?"

An ice-cold shiver prickles my neck before the hot flush rises to my temples. I'm already shaking my head when I say, "No. No, it wasn't Tom. Tom was the one that stopped it from happening."

"So he says." Kaitlyn clenches her jaw. "You've only got his word to go on. For all you know he could have stolen that identity. He could be ripping Pauline off. He could have false bank accounts. He might be after your money."

I'm beginning to wish I'd driven to Castleton on my own. Nicky's being exceptionally chatty, talking about how great it is to be spending the day doing something different, how she's still buzzing from the gig I did last night, how she hopes I'm still going to be around next week to perform again, how glad she is that I chose The Foundry to lodge in rather than one of those tacky chain hotels. Her chatter is all very nice. In normal circumstances, her demeanour and flattery would be inflating my ego and drawing me towards a desire to spend more and more time in her company.

"There's a very strong chance that I won't be here next week, you know?"

A momentary silence fills the car and Nicky casts me a sidelong glance. "What you really mean by saying that is, *this isn't a date, Nicky!*"

The grimace that comes to my face is involuntary and instantly regretted. "That obvious?"

"Yep, that obvious…" Nicky turns away, her gaze

fixed on scenery that flashes past the passenger window as she taps a monotonous beat on the glass with her freshly painted dark blue nails.

"Sorry. It's just—"

"You don't want me getting the wrong idea… It's cool. I get it. You're already taken."

The uncomfortable silence that smothered the car's interior dissipates as quickly as it descended. Nicky's suddenly all smiles again as she flicks off a shoe and draws a bare foot onto the seat.

You're so easy to spend time with, I think, knowing that if I am still here in a week's time, I'm going to find it increasingly hard to leave.

Right now, Penny is little more than a fictional character, even though while singing last night, I felt a strong connection to her. Last night I felt the bond associated with genuine memories, memories of actual events. Sitting here now, however, next to Nicky – breathing the aroma of her perfume, listening to her chat away with no ill feeling, with not the slightest hint that we just had a frosty moment, feeling relaxed, knowing that she's also completely relaxed in my company – those memories associated with Penny feel less real. They feel like they belong to somebody else, as if they are related to events that happened to another and I've learned of them third hand. I feel like a foot that's been slipped into a shoe that belongs to another person: it seems to fit, it appears to suit my taste, but it just doesn't feel quite right.

Not for the first time, I can't help but wonder what would have happened had I not written the journal, or if I'd not discovered it in the glove compartment, or if I'd simply refused to read it. I can't help but wonder what has happened during these missing weeks in past years. I can't help but wonder if I will remember taking this drive with Nicky. Will I wake up in Penny's flat one morning with no memory of this entire week? Will I have no memory of Nicky? Have there been others like Nicky in the past? I have no way of knowing. Maybe it will come to me in a surge of remembrance. Even if it does, without supporting evidence, how would I know it to be true? Thanks to the journal, this time I will remember. Thanks to the journal, I was encouraged to write everything down in a notebook, and I have done so. I've written down everything, including Nicky. Penny encouraged the writing of that journal, and thinking of her, possibly sitting at home, worrying about me, makes me determined to return to her. Even if I don't discover anything useful while I'm here, I will go back. I may not have true memory of a love for Penny, but it is surely there, as is her love for me.

"Just stick to this road all the way now," Nicky says, making me realise that I'd switched off and left her chattering to herself. She doesn't appear to have noticed.

Stick to this road, I think. *Don't wander from the path.*

We pass a sign that marks the next village as a place named Hope. I realise that hope is all I have to hold on to: hope that the words in the journal are true, hope that I actually do love Penny as much as the writing indicates, hope that she loves me equally, hope that I will feel it still if and when I do return, hope that my memories will return and not carry with them the burden of something I'd rather have left undiscovered. More than any of the residents of this village, I truly am living in hope.

"So, how's the family history thing coming along? This trip something to do with it?"

"I've not found much out, to be honest. Not yet, at least. I just want to go and see the cave because it's mentioned in the journal."

"Just curiosity, then?"

I guess curiosity just about sums it up, but then I recall sitting by the side of the church and recollect the memories that streamed into my mind.

"How come you don't know when you'll be leaving?" Nicky asks, without waiting for an answer to her prior question.

I glance over at Nicky to discover that she is looking out of the side window, just taking in the scenery as we move away from Hope and head towards the Devil's Arse of Castleton. She's just making small talk, not throwing high-pressure questions as I originally thought. "It's complicated."

"Ooo, now I'm intrigued," she gasps, turning from the window and fully fixing her attention on me.

As I see a car park ahead that proudly boasts a sign for the cave, I consider telling her an untruth. If the journal is to be believed, if this year pans out as others supposedly have done, Nicky will turn up for work one day to discover I've just disappeared without even having had the good grace to say farewell. She deserves better than that.

Not surprisingly, given that it's the cold month of January, the car park is relatively empty. I drive to the far end, stones pinging from under the tyres, and pull up near to a path that is signposted as leading to the Devil's Arse. Switching the engine off, I take a moment to think while gazing up at the ruined castle halfway between the bottom and the top of the hill. Unseen from here, the cave is directly beneath it.

I have to release a huff of amusement when I finally turn to look at Nicky. She's still facing me and is half kneeling, having drawn both feet onto the seat, a look of excited expectation painted on her face as if she's anticipating a gift-wrapped surprise of revelation.

"I can't say exactly when I'll be leaving because I truly don't know. I… have no control over it."

Nicky pulls back with a scowl that folds a sharp crease into the bridge of her nose. A wash of wide-eyed concern then stretches that crease of concern to invisibility. "Are you in some kind of trouble? Is someone after you? Is that why… you know… with the police?"

"No. No, nothing like that." How best to tell it. I give my chin a brisk rub and draw my jowls with fingers and thumb, marvelling at how quickly last night's clean shave has sprouted new growth. "I don't know who I am, and I don't know where I normally live." I grimace as I realise that the statement is not exactly true. "Well I kind of do, but… I'll come back to that in a bit. Like I said, it's complicated."

"Sounds it," she says, adjusting her posture to a position that's more suited to intent listening, a look of worry showing in her eyes.

"That lilac journal I carry around, well, it was apparently written by me."

"When you say, *apparently*…?"

"I mean I don't remember writing it. It says I have a girlfriend named Penny who I've been seeing for the past five and a half years. It also points out that she encouraged me to write it. It claims that I disappear for just over a week, every January, and that I return home with no recollection. So far, that part I can definitely believe, because I have no idea how or why I came to be in Sheffield."

"Bloody hell."

I raise my eyebrows in reply and release a huff of tension, feeling more and more pleased with every word uttered that I chose to share this information with her.

"Do you think you wrote it?"

"I think so. There's stuff in there that's… It says I play gigs at a local pub, that I can play guitar and sing, and, well, I guess last night showed that to be true."

Nicky chuckles and shakes her head, her distinctive sexy wry smirk forming on her lips. "So you really didn't know if you could play or not. That's a bit trippy. What about the little black note book?" she asks, her gaze flicking to the back seat, where it sits atop the lilac journal. Her gaze lingers on it for a moment as if she longs to have a read of both.

"I said it was complicated. Apparently, when I'm living this life with Penny, I can't remember the first twenty years of my life. Even the age is a bit of a guess, it seems, because I have no real way of knowing for certain. In the journal, I advise keeping a notebook during this disappearance in the hope that it might help me to remember the earlier years of my life."

Now it's Nicky's turn to puff her cheeks and release a lung-full of what? Incredulity? Disbelief? Concern? Empathy? "And is it… helping?"

"Not really. I think I might have grown up around Wincobank. It just… sort of feels right. There some references in the journal: descriptions and stuff from a nightmare. They align with places and buildings on the hill: the church and the recreation ground. Memories of being a child and playing in that area came to me when I was sitting in the car and looking around, but I don't know if they're real memories. How could I know, unless someone can back them up? How can you be certain that something really happened, unless you have someone with you that shared the event leading to the memory of it, or some other evidence, like photos or a video?"

Nicky looks towards the ruined castle through the windscreen that is gradually misting to the point where the outside world will be masked from view. Breaking from deep thought, she turns back to look at me. "I get what you mean. Kind of scary, really, when you think about it. I mean writing could be just made up, especially if you don't remember writing it."

"I found a photo of Penny tucked inside the journal, and one of me too, so that gives it a bit more credibility. I've written about everything that's happened over the past week, so I'm hoping I might remember writing it, as well as the things I've discovered during this week when or if I go back."

Nicky reaches across and gently runs her fingers over my cheek. Her lush lips curl into a warm sympathetic smile as she draws her comforting hand back to her lap. Her cheeks have flushed with either embarrassment or passion. "I can't even begin to imagine how you must feel, how you're coping. Why are you telling me…? I mean, why now?"

A big part of me wants to reach out for the hand that stroked a measure of comfort over my cheek, to hold it while we speak, but I resist the urge. "I like you, Nicky." My voice breaks slightly. I cough into my clenched fist as I look in the direction of the ruined castle. The windscreen has been completely obscured by the warm breath we've expelled. I then turn back to face the young woman sitting in the same car as me, sharing the same air as me, forming a memory of an event that we can both declare as being real. I've surely had this same feeling many times over with Penny, though. "If it wasn't for the journal, for the stuff that's written in there, we might... there'd have been nothing to stop me getting to know you better. It's because I like you that I'm telling you now. If the journal is correct, I'll just disappear, go back to Surrey and not even remember being here. If that does happen, I don't want you to think I purposefully left without saying goodbye. I don't want you to think bad of me." I feel the sharp sting of tears in my eyes, so I stop talking and turn to look at the driver's side window. I continue to look, despite the fact that the view out is completely obscured by mist.

"I want to write my phone number in your notebook."

Wiping the back of my hand across my right eye, catching the one tear that managed to escape, I sniff and turn back to face Nicky. "Why?" I ask as she takes hold of both my hands.

"Because when you get home, you're probably going to question whether the writing in the notebook is true. You're going to question whether you actually played a gig in a pub called The Foundry. You might wonder if you made it up. Like you said: how can you know for certain unless someone else shared the same event? You'll be able to ring me, and I'll be able to tell you that it's true, that it did happen. And, if things don't work out, if you remember who I am and where to find me, you might come back."

Her coy smile tells me that last line was partially in jest. The trace of sadness in her eyes as the smile wanes tells me it was also partially wishful. "If you really don't mind, I think that'd be a good idea."

* * *

"You okay?" Nicky asks.

I'm aware that my pace has slowed to the point where I've almost stopped walking. The path is approaching the point where it curves right around the cliff face, where it will then reveal an uninterrupted view of the cave entrance. My mouth has dried to the point where I'm finding it uncomfortable to swallow. My legs feel jelly-like.

"You look like you've seen a ghost or something."

It's only when Nicky takes hold of my hand that I

realise I've actually stopped progressing altogether. It's only through the heat of her skin that I realise how cold I feel. It's only through the steadiness of her grip that I realise I'm trembling.

"What is it?" she asks, the concern in her voice dragging my gaze from the curve in the path.

"I– I don't know." The tremble in my hand is also present in my voice. "I just feel afraid, but I don't know what of."

Nicky pulls me into an embrace, a hug that lasts long enough for the comfort it gives to fade into awkwardness. We draw apart and I feel like a drowning man that has just lost the very thing that was preventing him from slipping under and plummeting to dark and irretrievable depths. Nicky gives me an empathetic, slightly embarrassed smile and then takes both my hands in hers, gripping just the fingers, as if that is any less intimate. "What does the journal say about this place, exactly?"

"It says that I visited here with Penny last summer, and that I had a panic attack when I saw the cave entrance."

"No wonder you're bricking it then. You're expecting the same thing to happen, building it up in your imagination."

I nod, reflectively, as my gaze slowly drifts to the curve in the path, the point where the black cave entrance will come into view.

"We can just go back, if you like?"

Chewing the inside of my lip, slowly dragging my gaze back to look at Nicky, I pause for a moment, lost in her eyes, in the warmth of empathy that's looking back at me. "I just want to remember."

"Just take a moment."

Perhaps because the pressure to look upon the cave has been removed from me, a memory comes to mind of a young boy racing up the path with a younger girl chasing after him. The boy is laughing and so is the girl, but her laughter is filled with delightful cries of *slow down, Thomas. I can't keep up.* A middle-aged couple are walking up the path, hand in hand, and not too far behind. They are following the children, big smiles of pride etched on their faces.

"I think I might have visited here as a child, with my parents. And, I think I have a younger sister."

Nicky reflects my half-hearted smile. "That's good then… that you came here, I mean, if it's making you remember stuff. Do you want to…?"

I follow Nicky's line of sight as it steers up the path. I imagine the black cave entrance like a mouth, a void that swallows and extinguishes daylight within a few paces of its depth. The imagining chases a cold shiver down the length of my spine. "No… I don't think I need to see it. I… Let's go back to the car."

CHAPTER

2 4

Kaitlyn has put more doubt in my mind than I'm comfortable with. I want rid of it, the doubt. I need to know... I can't actually know; who can for certain? But, I need to believe that Tom is to be trusted. My belief remains, but it has been shaken. I'm hoping Mrs Gaskell can reinstate my faith in the man. There are two sides to any argument, and so far during Tom's current disappearance, the loudest, most common sense one has been Kaitlyn's. As well meaning as she is being, her view does not align with my own. I don't really know what I'm going to ask Mrs Gaskell, but I'm hoping she will say something to halt the growth that has sprouted from the seeds of doubt Kaitlyn has planted.

At the far side of Mrs Gaskell's expansive lawn stands the shed where Tom actually lived for a few weeks of his life. As I gaze in that direction I wonder where Tom is living right now, where he's sleeping and what he's doing right at this moment. I wonder where he is and hope he's okay. It's only recently that I learned of him waking on a London street with no knowledge of who he was, or where he came from, and I can't even begin to think how he felt back then. It enters my mind to wonder how on earth he coped, but if my theory of repressed memory is correct, that situation was likely the very thing that actually allowed him to cope.

If he hadn't been living here at that time, in this shed, I would now be a victim of rape. Kaitlyn's implanted seed stirs the doubt in my mind, but I know it was Tom that saved me that night. It was not Tom that tried to rape me. The fact that a man died on the towpath that night might be pure coincidence.

Knocking on Mrs Gaskell's door, still gazing at the shed and the tall fence beyond it, I can't help thinking that fate brought me and Tom together that night. I'm amazed that he managed to scale the fence and drop onto the other side without being heard.

"Hello, dear."

I didn't even hear the door open. Slowly, when I hear Mrs Gaskell's voice, I unsnag my vision away from the region of the shed, and the fence and the memory of what occurred on the other side, on the path it hides.

"Has he done his disappearing act again?" Mrs Gaskell casts a quick glance down the garden as she asks the question.

It enters my mind to say *yes*, to say more than a simple *yes*, but my voice sticks in my throat. I quickly replace words with a nod of confirmation.

"Well, you'd best come in, dear. It's mighty cold out here." The clouding of her breath confirms the fact.

The cloud hardly has a chance to dissipate before Mrs Gaskell turns into the house. I take a last look at the tall fence, and enter the large hallway to note that the old lady is already half way to the kitchen. For one so frail looking, she's incredibly spritely. It's a big house for such a fragile looking single woman. The hallway seemingly swallows her as she navigates its length. I shut the door against the frosty air and drop the latch. The resulting quiet wraps around me, a quiet that feels softened by the aroma of this house. Despite the fact that Mrs Gaskell lives alone, this house feels like a home. I've always thought that a house is just a building – that is what my family home felt like when Mum got sick – but a home is a feeling, it's a feeling that is created by the people or person who inhabits that building. My gran made her house feel like a home, and Mrs Gaskell makes this house feel like a home. I like her. I trust her. Whatever she says, though I still haven't determined what I'm going to ask, I will believe.

"Tea? Coffee?" Mrs Gaskell's questions echo up the stairwell and disappear on a landing that's dimly lit from a small window, where there sits the most ugly monkey doll. I've seen it before, when visiting with Tom, on a trip to the toilet. It captivated me with its ugliness and while I stared at it for what seemed an age, I wondered not only why someone would purposefully make something that looked so horrid, but also why she would keep such a thing.

Mrs Gaskell is looking at me from the kitchen doorway, waiting for me to take my eyes from the top of the stairwell and give her an answer. "Coffee's good, thanks."

This kitchen takes me back in time to a period when my gran was still alive, though it's much bigger than the kitchen that Gran had. It has the same comforting aromas of jam making and pickling and baking. There's a yeasty smell coming from the sourdough that Tom reckons is at least thirty years old. Apparently, it lives in a large jar in the pantry, growing like a lazy, lumpy creature before being split to make bread and left to regrow in readiness of the next loaf. These are homely smells that don't exist in most modern dwellings. I find them delightful. Hopefully there will be a slice of homemade cake on offer; there usually is. Some people bake only when they are expecting company, but people like Mrs Gaskell bake for the enjoyment of it. I really should visit her more often, especially as she is ninety this year; not that you'd know it to look at her. To see her move, you'd guess her to be younger. To look in her eyes, you'd guess her to be younger. Time has not been so kind to her complexion and her posture, however, and I'm guessing that she has issues with her bones. Tom visits a couple of times a week, but I find it difficult with work. I can't prevent a small smile from curling the corners of my mouth as I think of the surprise party that Tom has been arranging for her. She's going to hate it and yet love it at the same time. I hope he will return. This is the worst of it: not the fact that he disappears, but the worry that he won't come back.

"Not all sadness then?" Mrs Gaskell places two mugs of coffee onto the table and then heads for the larder. "Cake?"

"Mmmm. Please."

I hear jars clattering against each other, and tilt my head to see strings of onions swing from hooks. Mrs Gaskell appears with a round biscuit tin, upside down, so that the cake is on the lid. My gran used to do the same.

"Coffee and walnut, being as Tom's away. I'll make certain to bake his favourite for when he gets back."

Coconut cake. Tom's favourite is coconut. She's talking as if he's simply left for a week's worth of winter sun: some chance of that with no passport. The image in my mind of a cake sitting in wait, moulding to blue over time, increases the constant dread that niggles me with a worry that this will be the time when he doesn't come back. Maybe this will be the time he will have to start over again, aged twenty-nine, or thereabouts, in someone else's shed.

With a groan, Mrs Gaskell lowers herself onto the seat opposite me. As if we are on a seesaw, I stand and cut myself a large slice of her perfect looking cake.

It tastes as delicious as ever. "You really must teach me how to bake some time, Tom being such a fan of your cakes, and all…"

"I would love to dear. Something tells me you haven't called to discuss cake baking, though. So what is on your mind?"

It's so typical of her to get straight to the heart of the matter. "I have something I want to ask you. It's something to do with the journal that I got Tom to write. Well, something that I read in it."

Mrs Gaskell screws her lips and raises her brow. "I don't imagine much good will come from this journal dear. I never have, not from the day Tom told me about it. But he said he was happy to give it a try, so who am I to argue against it?"

"Anything's got to be worth trying, hasn't it?" Obviously, Mrs Gaskell doesn't think so, judging by the lack of an answer. "Are you aware that he doesn't know anything at all about the first twenty years of his life?"

Mrs Gaskell takes a slurp of her coffee, her wise eyes gazing at me from over the rim as she slowly tips the mug back to level and places it on the table.

"Well, twenty years is a guess, Penny, because he has no real way of knowing, not for certain."

"So you did know? How long have you known?"

"I had suspected from first knowing him, but I've known for certain since just before he moved in with you, dear." The old lady composes herself, sitting more upright in the chair as if she's in a court of law. "He was concerned, worried that you would find out. I told him to be honest from the outset, but he felt he would lose you. It's bound to come out eventually, I told him, and now it has. So that's that."

"I only found out last May. We had an argument. I wanted to go for a short break to Barcelona, and it all came spilling out."

Mrs Gaskell draws a long intake of breath that wheezes slightly as it fills her lungs. "I know," she says, looking into her lap. "Tom told me all about it."

"Does Tom tell you everything?" I sound angrier than I intended to, and immediately feel a pang of regret.

"He's confided in me ever since I discovered him in my shed. I take it to mean that he felt he could trust me. I've not always agreed with his decisions, dear, but I have always kept his confidence. I believe he has enough to cope with, without also having nobody trustworthy to talk to."

She looks rather hurt and I'm stirred with guilt. I didn't come here with the intention of having a go. "I'm sorry, Mrs Gaskell."

"Pauline," she corrects, punctuating the word with a tut of emphasis.

"He could have told me sooner, though. I'm glad he's told me. Better late than never. Certain things make more sense now that I know."

"I suppose it was the correct time for it to come out then, dear. Early in your relationship things may not have run so smoothly. Tom's told me that you want to get married someday, maybe have children. I don't think I'll be betraying his confidence too much by telling you that he desperately wants the same. He's afraid though, afraid that he may not be good enough for you, that there may be something in his past that would render him unworthy. He's also concerned that he might possibly have a genetic inheritance that would make fathering a child unwise. We can't know about genetics without knowing his family history or testing, but we both know in our respective guts that he's a good man, don't we? And journal or not, mystery past or otherwise, I believe we need to convince him of that."

I find myself nodding gently while fixating on the reflection of a large cake crumb that's missed my plate and settled on the dark polished wood of the old kitchen table. To the rear of me a clock ticks away its loud seconds. I eventually look up to see that Mrs Gaskell is watching me with a sympathetic expression on her face. *How much more do you know?* I can't help but wonder. *How many secrets have been told to you over the years?* There and then, I decide to keep to myself the real reason I came. There and then, I have a deeper understanding of Tom's dread, of taking the easier option and not risking the discovery of something you'd rather not have known all along.

"So, what's the real reason for your visit?"

Bloody hell; can she read minds? Pauline holds my gaze with her own, her enquiring eyes not deviating by even a fraction of a millimetre.

"Something that you read in the journal that you encouraged him to write is what you said. But you have yet to mention what that something is. I know it's not the argument, or the discovery of Tom's missing twenty years, because that unravelled in the May before he began writing the thing."

With a sigh, I decide to go ahead. "Tom had written about the time just before he moved into my flat. It seems he'd been talking to you about it and, among other things, you apparently said to him: *you are not the only one who has repressed memories.* From the context, I get the impression you meant me…" Mrs Gaskell's eyes are closed as tightly as her pursed lips, as if by not looking at me she can more easily ignore the words I've just uttered. Hesitantly, I continue. "I'd... like to know what you meant."

Slowly, her mouth relaxes and her wrinkled lids open to eyes that seem to be full of regret and sorrow. "He should not have written that. I shouldn't... It was a foolish slip of the tongue."

"So, you were referring to me?"

The pained look on her face is enough. With some advanced warning, she'd likely have hidden it well, denied whatever it is she knows, but there is something, and Mrs Gaskell is fully aware that I'm aware of that fact. Tom may have let it drop, but I get a feeling this is something important, something that brought a horrified look to her face when almost mentioning it to Tom, and I intend to find out what it is.

CHAPTER

2 5

Mrs Gaskell gazes straight through me, as if I were made of glass. The clock to my rear ticks away a steady, unfaltering beat that counts the slow moments of silence. "I'd just like to know what you meant, Mrs Gaskell."

"Penny, will you please call me Pauline."

Not in a trance-like state then. "Very well... Pauline. Will you please tell me what you meant when you said, *you are not the only one who has repressed memories?*"

She glances at her lap, gives a subtle shake of her head, and then looks me in the eye. "Trust me, dear, there are some things that you are better off not knowing."

"So you do know something about me?" No answer, just the blank stare again, aimed at the wall behind my seemingly invisible head. "If it's about me, surely I have a right to know. Whatever it is, it might not be as bad as you think it is."

"It is about you, and it was told to me in

confidence, and as I've already said, there are some things that you are better off not knowing."

"And would you say the same to Tom?"

"To an extent, yes. Yes, I would. The mind has ways of dealing with painful events. Slumber lets us forget it for the time we are asleep. Anything more painful needs to be locked away behind imaginary doors and forgotten. I believe that the mind knows when it can cope with such memories and decide for itself when it is safe to open such a door. I don't believe forcing this imaginary door is a good idea, for crowbars – physical or metaphysical – are bound to cause damage. However, let's assume this journal experiment of yours does work, that it ends up being a key and not a crowbar. Let us assume that Tom returns here with knowledge of his missing twenty or so years. What if he discovers things he doesn't like? The Tom I know is happy and generous and kind, and that's good enough for me. What is so wrong with shelving the life you've led up to a certain point, and starting over? Sounds a wonderful idea to me. To a certain extent, I've done such a thing myself. My memories are still with me, of course, but I had to continue as if I'd never had a son, pretend that he doesn't exist in order to soften the pain. I can think of times in my life where forgetting altogether would have been an ideal alternative to the sufferance of haunting memories."

"I do wonder… Pauline, if some part of you is afraid of Tom discovering a past that he might want to return to? Are you fearful that he might discover parents, siblings, a grandmother, and abandon you?"

"A little, maybe; aren't you? Are you not afraid of losing him? Maybe he has filled a hole in my life that my deserting son and grandson left. Even so, my main concern is for Tom. What if said discovery changes him, makes him miserable, or depressed, or even suicidal? He might come back with an altogether different personality. We have no way of knowing. Those memories were suppressed for a reason."

"Well now you're scaring me a little. The not knowing does make him miserable though. It's preventing him from getting on with his life, from doing things that he wants to do. He's described the not knowing as a constant hunger that can never be satisfied."

"I know. He's said similar things to me. And yes, I understand, of course he needs to know."

She's trying to steer away from my question by turning my thoughts fully onto Tom. "So what about me?"

Mrs Gaskell rolls her eyes and then looks in my general direction, but without fully making eye contact. "Your situation is nothing like Tom's," she states, pausing with a pained grimace. "He knows there's a big chunk of his past missing."

"And I don't, you mean?"

"You didn't... And it isn't a big chunk."

"But there is something missing, you reckon... in my memory?"

"I knew your grandmother..."

Mrs Gaskell releases the sigh of someone defeated and now given over to the inevitable surrender. She looks at me with an expression of sorrow, as if pleading for release. I look back with what I hope is an expression that says, *I'm sorry, but now I know there is something to know, I'd like to know what that something is.* "My gran. Yes, I know you did. I recall her talking to you in the street. I used to find you scary."

"Really! Why?"

"You were so serious and stiff. All the kids knew you were headmistress at a posh school. There were rumours that you used to take pleasure from whipping the pupils that were naughty." I can't help but smirk in response to her horrified expression. "You once told me off for fidgeting, and when I looked at Gran for support she just raised her brows, as if to say, don't ask me to step in."

Mrs Gaskell exhales a huff of amusement and gently nods her head, her eyes distant as if visualising the scene. "Can't help the upbringing that moulds you, I guess. When your mother was ill, your grandmother visited me many times. She needed to talk, and she knew I'd listen. She also knew I'd keep what she had to say to myself. I would much prefer to keep her confidence, even though she's passed on…"

I keep quiet, allowing her pause to linger. Mrs Gaskell gently chews the inside of her cheek. The clock loudly ticks and tocks the passing seconds.

"… My father once took me to a travelling fair," she says, without warning or preamble. "He was a strict man, and wouldn't allow me any of the sticky delights on offer. He said of the whole fair that I could spend on one thing only. I chose the lucky dip, thinking that at least it came with the guarantee of a prize, and I would have something to keep. Everyone wins on a lucky dip. Now that I am older and wiser, I know that winning covers a broad spectrum of definition. There were two tea chests, one filled with shredded pink paper, and one filled with shredded blue paper. Naturally I chose the pink chest. I handed the man my coin, and delved deep into the chest, rummaging around for the biggest parcel I could find. *Happy?* Father questioned, when he saw my huge smile. That smile quickly faded when I unwrapped the parcel and discovered the ugliest monkey doll you're ever likely to see."

My eyes involuntarily drift to the hallway.

"Yes, the one that sits in the landing window. Father made me keep it, despite my tears. The man offered to exchange the hideous article, but Father would hear none of it… Why do you think I'm telling you this story, Penny?"

"You're saying that with a lucky dip you're always going to get something, but there's no guarantee you are going to like what you get."

"Exactly. Diving into the knowledge I hold is like plunging your hand into a lucky dip. And trust me dear, please do, you are not going to like what you pull out. And just like that monkey that father made me keep on my dresser, there will be no putting that knowledge back."

Mrs Gaskell looks out of the window, at the darkening sky. I'm wondering if she knows that I was almost raped in the lane out there, and if the glance is a gentle nudge for me to consider leaving for home before the very last of the daylight beats me to it. The lane no longer worries me, I have a car outside and I'll be driving home. She places the biscuit tin base over the cake, as if that is a signal that all is done here. Her anecdote may have been food for thought, but is hasn't sated my hunger.

"I'd still like to know," I say, as she begins to rise from the chair, "if you'll tell me."

With a groan and a sigh she lowers herself back to the seat. "Are you certain…? Can I say nothing that will induce you to change your mind? There will be no putting it back, and you'll have an ugly monkey of your own… Very well. What do you recall of your father's death?"

CHAPTER

2 6

"My dad disturbed someone who had broken into our house. I came downstairs just after the burglar had stabbed him and fled. Mum was already on the telephone, ringing for police and an ambulance. He'd bled out before the ambulance arrived." I'm puzzled to see Mrs Gaskell shaking her head. "Whaa…t?"

"I imagine that to be a most horrible memory, Penny, one you'd rather not have, one that has maybe caused you to envy Tom's situation a little?"

"A little, yes, I suppose."

"Do you still wish me to continue?"

Holding the gaze of those wise old eyes, I gently nod that, yes, I would like her to continue.

"There are circumstances to do with the burglary incident that you have repressed, my dear. The memory you have is ugly, but not as ugly as the one you've locked behind a metaphysical door."

"No," I say, shaking my head. "That's exactly what happened. I remember it as clear as anything, as clear as if it happened only yesterday."

"Tom told me you have done some research into complications with the mind's capacity for reliably archiving events of the past. I would have thought you'd be more open to the issue of unreliable memories. I would imagine unreliability is more common than the extreme memory problems you suspect Tom has. His memories are completely lost to him; yours are merely altered. I don't know about Tom, because I don't know what he will discover, but I know for certain that your altered memory is protecting you from something worse. I urge you to leave it at that."

"Maybe you've got it wrong. That night is clear in my mind. It definitely happened as I remember it."

"Then why not simply accept it as being so?"

"Because you've piqued my curiosity, now. When you tell me what you think you know, I'll then be able to dismiss it and move on. It's like knowing you've locked a door and someone putting doubt in your mind; until you check, you can't really settle. That night has to be as I remember it. Surely, if it wasn't, if I'd invented something, it'd be kind of fuzzy, or it would keep altering a little."

"I think the opposite is more likely. The invention, if firmly planted, if it exists as a barrier, will likely be more concrete." Pauline pauses for a long while, a puzzled looking expression on her face that indicates she is thinking hard about something. "I recall reading some research that was carried out in regard to how reliable memory is… maybe it was a TV documentary, or radio…? Where it came from is of little importance. A group of people were invited to watch, among other things, a traffic accident that took place at a road junction. Later in the day they were individually asked questions in regard to the various tests and film clips. Of the traffic accident, they were asked who was to blame. Every single one of them said the red car, which incidentally was the first to be hit. The researchers said, *what about the white van that jumped the red light?* Each and every person claimed to have not seen the white van. A year later, the same people were interviewed about the traffic accident and all the other things that had been part of the experiment. They were again asked, *who was to blame for the accident?* Every single one of them said it was the fault of the white van that had jumped the red lights. More than half of them could not recall the colour of the car that was the first to be hit. It was then revealed that there had not been a white van. Despite seeing the video again and confirming that fact, the people who had taken part were convinced that they had seen a white van. They found it difficult to believe that the memory had been implanted. Not only did they believe that the white van truly existed, it was the strongest memory of the day, much stronger than the memory of the red car that truly did exist."

"And this is relevant, because…?"

"Because there was no burglar, dear. The burglar is your white van. Your mother told you there was an intruder, a burglar, and you accepted it as being true. You also didn't come down stairs when you heard a disturbance; you were already down stairs."

"But… I saw… If there was no burglar, who stabbed my dad?"

"There were only three people in your house that night, Penny, and it wasn't you. Your father didn't stab himself, so that leaves only one other."

"The police came. They believed there was a burglar."

"Your mother must have been very convincing. Your grandmother told me that your mother had hidden the knife and had thrown it in the canal the next day."

Now it's Mrs Gaskell that has an invisible head, and I am the one that's staring at a wall, the clock loudly ticking and tocking to my rear.

My stomach flips with a sickening rush of memory that comes to mind in a seemingly altered timeline of order. I'm standing in the living room, looking out into the hallway. I see Dad in an expanding puddle of blood, Mum with a knife in her hand, screaming at me to go up stairs to my room. She pauses slightly as she looks into the kitchen, and then yells, *NOW! The burglar might come back*. Next thing I'm being carried downstairs by Dad. Then we're in the living room, him telling me that we're going to play our secret game, when mum bursts in and starts yelling at him. She tells me to go to my room, calmly this time. I see a knife behind her back as I look over my shoulder from the hallway. I climb the stairs and crawl into my bed, tears rolling onto my pillow. I hear them yelling, and creep back down stairs, clutching my old bear. They're standing at the bottom of the stairs. Dad falls, clutching his stomach. Mum yells at me to go to my room.

Mrs Gaskell was correct; I don't like what I've pulled out. It's ugly, but it is at least still partially wrapped. Finer details are still hidden to me and I can keep it that way, I can do that by not unwrapping my ugly monkey any more than I already have done. For all I know, without Mrs Gaskell's confirmation, this stream of imagery could be invention that has been generated from my worst fears. There is no knowing what the exact truth is without corroboration, and there is a woman sitting opposite to me who can do just that.

If this recollection is a true account, if Mum did implant a burglar in my memory, I can think of only one reason for why the chain of events I've just imagined would have pushed Mum into stabbing Dad. I'm not going to ask Mrs Gaskell to confirm my suspicion. I'm going to keep my monkey tightly wrapped.

"I don't want to know any more."

Mrs Gaskell nods her approval, leans across the table, and pats my hand. "I think that's wise, dear."

Have all of us got repressed memories? I now wonder. *Do we all invent alternate realities that somehow allow us to cope? If we do, how would we know?* Maybe I shouldn't have suggested for Tom to write the journal after all. I now dread to think what kind of memories he might unearth. Tom believes he will be happier knowing, even if he discovers something bad. So did I.

I was mistaken.

I have to believe that Tom is a good man. I have to believe that even in the worst of situations he would do the right thing. Whatever has been repressed though, might not be something bad that he did, but something bad that was done to him by another. Thinking about the possibility of my mum throwing a murder weapon into the canal, I need to ask Mrs Gaskell if she knows about the one thing that has bothered me ever since Tom climbed her fence and came to my rescue.

"Do you know that I came close to being raped, when I was seventeen, on the lane that runs down to the canal?"

Mrs Gaskell rises from her chair with a groan, and ambles across the kitchen on slightly bowed legs. She turns on the light and comes back to the table. Not until she is seated does she say, "Yes, dear, Tom told me."

"When?"

"He told me about preventing a rape years ago, not long after it had happened, but only in the year just gone did he tell me that the girl was you."

"I didn't go to the police. I just ran home to Gran's. The next day, they found the body of a young man in the canal, in one of the docks. His neck had been broken."

Mrs Gaskell's eyes fix on mine, and she sits in silence.

I quietly ask the same question that I've secretly asked many times before. "I've often wondered if it was the man that tried to rape me. I didn't get a look at him, you see. Do you think Tom would be capable of doing that?"

"No, I don't believe he would be."

"What did he tell you about that night?"

"Tom told me that he had prevented a man from raping a girl. Said he chased the man along the canal, but the man was faster than him. Said he gave up the chase and went back to see if the girl was all right. She'd already gone when he got back."

"What if Tom did catch him? What if…?"

"What if? What if? Do you really want to know? Tom says he chased the man along the canal, and that the man got away. It's muddy on the towpath. Always is in winter. Maybe the man was panicking, sprinting for all he was worth, looking over his shoulder to see if he was still being chased. Maybe he's thinking that Tom is still there, chasing, not giving up. Maybe the man stumbles or slips. Maybe he hurtles into the balance beam of the dock gate. Maybe the impact breaks his neck and the momentum of the fall carries him into the lock. Maybe he's already dead before he hits the water. Maybe Tom sees it happen, and the man is not splashing about, and there's no point in trying to save him. Those locks are deep, and at that time of year near to freezing."

I can't help but think Mrs Gaskell is implanting a burglar or a white van in my mind, but I grab it with thanks, and simply nod in response to the scenario she has painted. "Pauline, do you think I could sleep here, tonight?"

"There's nothing I'd like more," she says, a warm smile colouring her face.

CHAPTER

2 7

Darkness has already descended as we pull into The Foundry's car park, despite my speeding along country lanes. Momentarily I regret stopping off for a bite to eat on the way back from Castleton. But had we not, the reason I wanted to get back before nightfall might not have come to my mind. While Nicky chatted, my mind wrestled with the surfacing memories of growing up with a younger sister. Many of those memories, I think, were created on the hill where I'd had first woken in the car.

"I'm going to have to quickly shoot off home, or I'll be late for my shift," Nicky says while checking her watch.

"Want me to run you?" I'm feeling slightly distracted, and glancing up at the hill as I ask the question.

"Quicker if I walk," she informs me. "You'd have to take the long way, and it's only a couple of streets in that direction."

A part of me is pleased that she doesn't want a lift, as I'm desperate to confirm the fragments that have been presented to me in the memories of playing near the top of the hill. "You sure?"

"Yeh. No worries. See you in the bar, later?"

I'm desperately struggling to hold on to what I hope are true recollections, and it's only when I notice that Nicky is on the opposite side of the road giving me a casual wave, that I realise she had asked me a question. Maybe I answered without realising, but I think not, and rush to get out of the car. "See you later," I shout as she turns away, causing her to turn back and wave again.

"Yeh, later." There's a chuckle in her voice that tells me she was amused by the incident. The fact that she shows such a response fills me with warmth and brings a smile to my face as I watch her jog away.

It's already dark out, so the rush to be back has abated somewhat. After writing down the events of the day, and the memories that they brought to mind, I switch on the kettle and pick up the journal, intending to read a few pages while warming up with a cup of tea. There aren't many pages left to read, and much of what I've read recently is just a general account of everyday life that has encouraged me to begin skimming the text. There's some mention of booking a room for a surprise party for Mrs Gaskell's 90th birthday next year. There is also mention of shopping for Christmas presents for Penny, which goes on to say how much I think she's going to like what I've bought. That Christmas has already passed. I've already spent it with Penny. I've already given her the gifts, whatever they were, and I have absolutely no recollection of either buying them, giving them, or of whether she was elated or disappointed when she opened them.

I'm too distracted to take in any more of the journal, so I place it on the bed and drink the last of the tea. The journal and all it speaks of has begun to bore me, and thinking about how much I'm looking forward to seeing Nicky in the bar later, I can't help but wonder if I find my life with Penny boring. According to the writing, I don't, and I suppose reading about something is a lot different from living it, but I don't feel it. I wish I did.

I've been in this situation before, though, supposedly.

Were it not for the journal, I would not be aware of Penny right now. There would be only Nicky. I like her. I more than like her. For that reason, knowing what I know from reading the journal, I will not allow the friendship I've developed with Nicky to advance towards anything else. It has only been a few days, after all. That probably says something about how much I'm attracted to her. I want to take it to the next level. I really want to. But I won't. Had it not been for reading the journal I likely would have, and for that I am both grateful and resentful in equal measure.

There's nothing preventing me from enjoying her company while I am here though, and I feel a flip of child-like giddiness at the thought of doing so. Thinking of spending more time with Nicky, I realise that I stink. Maybe I should have bought more than one pair of jeans and one tee shirt. A shower is most definitely called for, which means either putting on smelly soiled clothes or wearing the dark suit. I was going to explore the hill, look for evidence that the memories of playing on the hill have actually got some substance to them. I could look tomorrow, when it gets light, but who's to say I will still be here. Tomorrow might be the day when I wake up on a sofa in Surrey.

Grabbing the car keys, snatching the journal and notebook from the bed, I head for the door. Then I hesitate. I have a strong compulsion to shower and change first.

CHAPTER

2 8

Sitting in the car, at the exact spot where I woke on that first day, I glance at the vista of twinkling lights before consulting my notebook. I can't be completely certain that I am at the correct part of the hill, but the landmarks and the curvature of the hill where the side avenue meets it would suggest I am. The complication, therefore, is the bank of houses to my left: a cul-de-sac that is four houses deep. When the memory came to me earlier on, the area of land occupied by the houses was empty scrubland. I visualised it as a makeshift playing field where the local kids would fly kites and play cricket, where they would kick balls and ride bikes. A distinctive feature of that very memory though, something that would evidence it as genuine if it were still in existence, is a large brick and concrete platform that sits at the far reach of the flat area and overlooks the natural slope of the hill.

Maybe it stands there still, hidden from view,

behind the houses.

With that thought comes a blast of memory, words this time in the voice of a child: *meet you at the concrete stand after tea.*

With the strong impression of riding a bike over the undulations of land where modern houses have sprouted, I clamber out of the car and look for the best way to get around them. There is an area further up the hill that has not been built on, and setting off in that direction, I assume there is a possibility of getting to the land behind the houses.

The air has a harsh bite this evening, the kind of cold that generates frost and transforms shallow puddles to deathly patches of invisible ice. Along a path with a pungent aroma suggestive of lazy dog-walkers I make my way by the topmost edge of the small clutch of houses. Where the fences of the last houses lie, the path curls away and climbs up the hill. I need to move away from the path and follow the rear of the gardens. The land is overgrown, its tangle having flourished in summer, laid dormant in autumn, and hardened to vicious thorn over winter. Only halfway to my projected goal at the mid-point of the cul-de-sac's rear, my hands are scratched and scraped where I've attempted to protect my suit from bramble snags.

This is the place, I realise as my feet step onto something solid and completely flat. Weeds have flourished where childhood experience had blossomed. The words, *gun-stand,* enter my head. *Gun-stand,* not, *concrete stand.* I recall it being part of a class project on World War Two. Several of these were built on the hill and sported large guns to protect the steel works from the planes that wished to lay them flat. I huff at the thought, as I crouch at the edge, rocking back on my heels. I close my eyes and try to remember what it looked like when I was young. Where bombs had failed, commerce in the shape of a shopping mall combined with cheap steel from abroad has succeeded.

A sharp gust tugs at my suit and I regret leaving my leather coat in the car. My hands ache from the cold bite. I rub the surface and wince as the gashes sting like buried needles. I need to empty my bladder. I could return to the pub and use the lavatory there, but I'm not yet ready to leave this spot. The houses are close by, but a glance over my shoulder confirms that I'm hidden in darkness. Unless someone else is crazy enough to scramble through bramble nobody is going to see me, so I just get on with it, turning my back to the wind, sighing with the relief of my steaming release.

A memory hits me with such strength that I almost piss down my leg. I'm standing at the edge of the gun-stand, one boy to the right of me, another to the left. We're urinating, seeing who can pee the furthest distance down the hill. A gust of wind twists towards and across us, moving from left to right. It catches my spray and pelts it into the boy on the right of me. The other boy and I roll about on the gun-stand, crying tears of laughter as he spits and complains that it went in his mouth. The memory feels so real, so vivid, and with this recollection of pissing in the wind, I feel that I no longer am.

But maybe I've been here before. Maybe I've remembered this before and then forgotten it. The notebook will prevent that from happening again, I realise, whipping it out and scribbling the words down on paper that is lit by the light of a frosty moon. Tucking the notebook back into my pocket I glance at the moon and envisage a zero with a piece missing. It's an odd memory that seems unattached to anything.

I shake away the ruined zero, and look around the hill, hoping more memories will come. Surely I grew up here, on this very hill. I can see the church from the gun-stand, and the cark space that is occupied by the recreation ground just below. The memories of playing in both of those places come back to me. The two boys of that recollection were likely the same ones as were with me on the gun-stand. I see us on the gun-stand again, sitting down, leaning against pushbikes. We're telling stories of bravery and invented exploits and mischief, and calling one another liars, and as darkness descends so our need for devilment rises. *Black Bend Bridge,* one of us cries, to the shrill agreement of the other two.

In the memory, the three boys – me in the centre, one on my right, and one on my left – cycle fast over the undulating ground where houses now reside, heading for the road that descends the steep hill. In reality, I rush through undergrowth that snags and snares and struggles to stop my progress. Rushing to the car with as much speed as I can muster, I worry that the memory is cycling too fast for me to keep up.

CHAPTER

2 9

The imagined boys on bikes are waiting for me when I get back to the car. They're standing astride the crossbars with both feet on the ground, hands on the grips in readiness of racing down the hill towards Black Bend Bridge. I'm sitting in a car, the excitement of an eleven-year-old rolling in my gut. I may be sitting in a car, looking down a hill, but I'm also the boy in the middle of the three. While they wait for their courage to rise, I wait for the melting of frost from the windscreen.

We each lean back, and like astronauts preparing for take off, press our dynamos into contact with the rear tyres. And then we're off, peddling for all we're worth, cycling down the hill at breakneck speed, dynamos whirring the lights to brilliance, Jack to the left of me, and Martin to the right of me. Speed gathered we enjoy the delight of freewheeling. Wanting the same level of exhilaration, the sensation of flying, I slip the car into neutral and allow gravity to pull it down the hill. I wind down both of the front windows and enjoy the whirl of cold harsh wind whipping my hair. "Look no hands," I shout, letting go of the wheel, grabbing it with heart-jolting alarm as the bikes bank around the bend where the shops jut out in defiance of the steep slope, Jack slightly in front, Martin drawing level, and a strange sensation of someone else, or something else behind. It's the fear, I tell myself, glancing over my shoulder. The fear is following. The fear of a car coming the opposite way; the fear of a pedestrian stepping into the road; the fear of falling off at this outrageous speed. Fear can't quite catch up though; we're outrunning fear. Fear will be with us soon enough, when we look down onto Black Bend Bridge.

Extra speed now, chin to handlebar, peddling furiously in top gear, dynamo whizzing the bulb to its ultimate brightness. The road runs straight now, steep and true from here to the river at the bottom. We fly past the church, hurtle past the red rec, and brake hard for the junction, pads squealing in protest as we pass The Rising Sun, its drinkers hidden behind pebbled glass. The skinny bike tyres almost slide from beneath us, as we take a sharp ninety-degree right into a road that travels parallel to the wall that plummets a forty-foot drop to the railway line.

Time has changed this hill. Traffic lights flare a commanding red on what was once an open junction.

I slip the gearbox from neutral to second. The car lurches in protest, gears not in synch with the speed. The Rising Sun has long ago been demolished. Where the public house and a row of back-to-back houses once stood, there is now a flat and open car park to accommodate a small factory that has replaced the rest of the out-dated housing. I can see that the main road is clear as I approach at speed. I don't want the memory to cycle away from me, and the memory is trying its utmost. The red light is helping it to get away from me. The memory is already cycling fast along the main road, following the railway wall on its way to Black Bend Bridge. With a squeal of tyres, I jerk the steering to the right, and run the red light, ramming the accelerator to the floor, leaving a cloud of smoke and a stench of burning rubber in my fishtail wake.

My heart thumps like a drum, its pulsing beat throbbing my temples with a frightful heat.

The road is coming up on my left. I feel that the bikes turned down there, though I do not see them. I turn a sharp left and slam on the anchors. There it is: Black Bend Bridge. Excitement and fear play a part in making my blood surge as I look into an opening as black as a starless sky. The boys have outrun me, the image of them gone, but the memory of them rattles in my mind all the same.

A shudder runs through me as I remember the shadows in the gas works that once stood on the right.

I hear the deafening hammers behind the tall black corrugated-wall on the right. I see the forgotten image of what to me at the time was dragon flame glimmering through gaps when the molten steel was poured. Steam would billow through those gaps: brimstone from the dragon's lair. A mist would always coalesce around the black entrance, cold air meeting the pipe rendered hot from the steel-cooling water and generating a strange microclimate. Magic, we thought at the time: a magic cloud to hold back the evil, to prevent it from leaving the void.

The pipe is no longer there, for the steelworks are silent and dead. An eerie mist floats before the void all the same. A puddle, perhaps frozen to a black mirror of ice, reflects the stone of the arch that is brightly lit by the light of a full and frosty moon. Perhaps the hot pipe had nothing to do with the creation of the mist. Perhaps it has more to do with the dip of the road and the heavy stone of the void breathing its frigid death-like breath into the night.

I'm an adult sitting in a car, not a kid standing astride a bicycle. I'm rational. I have no reason to fear a narrow arched railway bridge that swallows the road. There is danger in it, for certain. Even as a rational adult I can see that, but I do not see the kind of stuff that children are afraid of. There's no bogeyman, there's no devil, no dragon, no evil, no monsters, just the threat of hitting an oncoming car if it were going too fast. The curve of the brickwork arch narrows the useable width, making it a squeeze for two cars. My memory calls it Black Bend Bridge, but it's more of a tunnel really. Perhaps forty feet long, it curves to the left before straightening out. That is the reason it looks so black. The other side cannot be seen, and if memory serves, which it seems to be doing, tall walls of black brick rise on either side of the exit, creating a light-blocking illumination-stealing canyon.

Sitting in the car, looking down into that black void, I feel as if hammers are pounding in my chest. The steel beating hammers have died. The thump is my heart, and it's beating so hard it feels like it's bashing my ribs. I'm trying to convince myself that I'm not afraid. I am afraid. I'm as afraid as when I was eleven, both feet on the ground, the crossbar of my bike leaning against my leg, Jack to the left of me, and Martin to the right.

The idea was to click the dynamo away from the tyre and ride through Black Bend Bridge with no lights. The idea was to pedal at speed through the curve of the tunnel in absolute darkness. I don't think I ever did it, though I can't be certain. I don't think Jack or Martin ever did it either. We'd just stand at the top of the slope, goading each other, calling each other yellow and chicken, flapping our elbows and clucking like fools against a background cacophony of hammers on steel.

An older boy once did it. Turned up with his mates while we were standing there. His mates had already done it, they claimed, backing each other up and making him feel small. The darkness swallowed him, as the hammers pounded and the dragon fire roared, and then we waited an age for him to return the long way around: along the bottom road by the river, up the hill a way, across the bridge, and back to us via the road that runs parallel to the railway line. *Nowt to it,* he'd said, bravery inflating his chest, contradicting a face drained completely of colour.

Sitting there, in the car, the engine quietly ticking, headlights illuminating the stone that formed the arch but being swallowed by the void, I decide that I'm going to do it, now, in the car. Through the open window a cold silence seeps. I turn off the lights and a glassy pool that covers the entire width of the road throws its reflection of the arch into sharper contrast, seemingly making from it a complete circle of black.

I'm an adult, not a fear-filled child.

I'm going to do it.

My heart rate steps up a gear as I press the clutch pedal to the floor and slip the car into first. With a blip of the throttle, I float my hand to the handbrake. Cold air pinches my cheeks. Hot beads of sweat trickle down my temples. Hammers pound as the rev-counter swings. I gulp and flex my grip of the brake. With slow deliberation, I press the button and lower the lever. Reflected light glazes the width of the road and creeps what little distance it can into the opening. Before fully releasing the lever, on the cusp of the point where the car would start to roll down the slope, I pause and drag the handbrake back against its protesting ratchet.

I guide the gears back to neutral. The cold night air pinches my cheeks, and the breeze seems to whisper, *chicken.*

I'm about to try again, when my eyes snag on a movement in the floating mist. I lean forward better trying to focus my eyes, as the icy breeze carries a tearful sob to my ears.

CHAPTER

3 0

Almost lost to shadow at the edge of the tunnel there sits a young girl, her knees drawn tight against her chest and her face buried in her hands, her shoulders shuddering as she sobs.

Dreading to think what would have happened if I had set off down the slope and driven through Black Bend Bridge at speed with the lights off, all thought of being eleven leaves my mind. Turning on the car headlights, I release the handbrake and allow the car to roll quietly down the slope. The breaks emit a squeal as I draw level. The girl looks up with a start, her expression tight with anxiety. I give her a big smile but realise that the car's interior is completely dark so she won't have seen my friendliness. I lean across the passenger seat, the seatbelts resistance forcing a staggered progress to the window.

She looks at me, wide-eyed, no-doubt afraid. A slight-looking thing, I guess that she can only be seven or eight at the most. She's wearing jeans that are frayed at the knee, and a very thin jacket. She looks perished to the bone, her cheeks drained of colour.

"I don't think you should be out here, alone." I'm not certain that the cheeriness I press into my voice actually works and the echo that the void throws back sends a shiver down my own spine. "There's rats as big as cats in there," I say, forcing a chuckle, tipping a casual nod of my head to the tunnel.

"They left me." Her voice cracks around the edge of a fresh sob. "I don't know how to get home."

"What's your name?" I ask, opening the door, trying still to sound as friendly and unthreatening as possible. "Mine's Tom."

"Emily," she says with a shudder that is driven by either the shelved sobbing or the cold, more than likely both.

"Emily? That's a nice name." I'm not certain I heard correctly, so quietly did she speak, but she doesn't contradict my repeating of the name so I guess I got it right. "Want to jump in? It's nice and warm in here."

I note that she draws both of her arms defensively around her body while giving me a blank stare, no doubt running through her mind all of the times she has been told not to get in a stranger's car. I consider asking her for a telephone number, then immediately realise that I don't have a mobile. I raise my eyebrows questioningly, and straighten my wide beaming smile to something less sinister.

Gradually, she moves from the cold kerb, swiping away her tears as she stands. She glances into the dark void, glances up the hill, and then looks back at me, a picture of worry painted on her face.

"You getting in then?"

Emily tips her head into a barely perceptible nod and approaches the open door, her arms out to the side for balance as she walks over the frozen puddle. She pauses momentarily, and then flops into the seat, where she sits and stares straight ahead at the gaping mouth of Black Bend Bridge.

She feels colder than the air outside the car. It's as if someone has just chucked a hunk of frozen animal onto the seat. She's so cold that I half expect to see a cloud of dry ice ripple from her skin. "You're like death warmed up," I say, before cranking the heat to high and leaning across her to close the door. "How long have you been out here?"

"Don't know," she says, her voice weak and flat. Twisting a strand of hair around her finger she turns to me with a nervous, slightly faltering smile, her eyes glassy with tears. "My brother left me."

I'm sure there will be more to it, but I leave it alone. That's one for her parents to question. "Right then, let's get you home, Emily. Where d'you live?"

"Ten Sycamore Avenue."

There's a distant tone in her voice that follows the

search in my mind for the familiarity of the address. "Oh, I know where that is" I tell her when realisation dawns. "Near the top of the hill, Right?" It's the very road I was parked across from mere moments ago when I went searching for the gun-stand, the spot where I woke in the car on the morning I arrived here. "We'll have you with your mum in no time."

Mention of her mum seems to give Emily the kind of reassurance that brings a warm smile to her face. It quickly dissolves however, as she turns back to look into the void. There's a look of fear etched on her face. It's a look I can identify with, as I look into the blackness myself while fumbling for the gear-stick. I crunch the transmission in my haste to select reverse, neglecting to fully depress the clutch pedal. The rev counter swings when I press the throttle, my eyes drowning in the void's depth, my memory swimming through the memory of hounding hammers and fearsome flame and searing steam as I look at the wall of cold and rusting corrugated steel. The car slides from side to side on black ice that spans the entire width of the road. I apply more revs, and hear the tyres slipping amid the engine's whine. I glance at the gear stick to make certain it's in reverse; at these revs, if I'd mistakenly selected first gear we'd career into the wall if the tyres were to suddenly grip.

And then they do grip.

The car lurches backwards. I fling an arm across

Emily's chest, preventing her from flying into the dashboard, and I struggle one-handed to bring the car into line. Dropping the revs to a more reasonable level, I reverse steadily to the top of the slope, the gears whining in high-pitched protest, my eyes fixed on the void, a whisper of *chicken* in my mind, *chicken* on the ice cold breeze, as I steer away from the void and turn onto the main road.

"Might be best if you fasten the seat-belt," I say, one eye on the road, another on the petrified girl who stares straight ahead and makes no move towards the belt. I decide not to push the matter and be sure to avoid any harsh braking.

"I think I used to live around here," I tell Emily as I pass through the traffic lights where the Rising Sun once stood. *Maybe I went to that school,* I think, as I glance in the rear-view mirror. "I think I used to play in there," I say, as we pass by the recreation ground and the church. "Do you play there?" She says nothing, just looks straight ahead as if in a trance. A flash of memory flares in my mind — cycling with a bag full of newspapers as I pass by the shops that jut in defiance of the steep portion of the hill. I'm forced to select a lower gear when I reach the steeper section of hill, because of allowing the revs to drop away.

Emily sits quietly in the passenger seat, still looking straight ahead, her eyes fixed on the road as we climb. *Number ten,* I remind myself, with a strong sense of deja vu. Emily turns to me and smiles a true smile as we turn onto Sycamore and pull up in front of the house bearing that number.

"This it?" I ask.

Emily turns to me with an expression of puzzlement. "I think so."

Thinking it strange that she would be uncertain, and feeling somewhat responsible for her, I open the door and get out of the car. I lean back in, and offer her what I hope is a reassuring smile. "You wait here a sec, Ems, I'll go and ask."

Walking up the steps is like trudging through wet clay. The steps are dry, however, and made of concrete, so any resistance is surely within me: my mind or my muscles refusing to co-operate. The paint on the door is peeling slightly. In the light of the streetlamps it is hard to determine the colour, other than it being a dark shade of paint. The number of the house stands out in stark contrast: white plastic numbers, a portion of the zero is missing, making it look like a back-to-front letter-c. With some trepidation, my arm trembling, I lift my hand to knock.

As my knuckles make contact, a new memory rips into my mind.

CHAPTER

3 1

The glass panels of the door flick from black to brilliant white, the swirling obscure shapes moulding the hallway's contents to indeterminable blobs of colour. Someone heads towards the door, and as they reach a hand forward an instinctual sense tells me to walk away. I don't. I stay there, standing, the frightful memory filling me with dread, waiting as a key turns in the lock. It sounds overly loud in the silence of the night. The door opens and a woman stands on the threshold looking out at me, the faint trace of a smile on a face that somehow looks older than it probably should. Weary, is probably a fitting description.

Shrouded in a veil of icy breath, her hands folded into opposite sleeves of a stretched cardigan, she rubs away the doorstep-chill. As she gathers folds of faded wool, I can't say which frightens me the most, the look in her eye, or the realisation. The realisation, as it prickles up my spine. Or the words. The words that, somehow, I know she is going to say.

They're words I don't want to hear.

I talk first, quickly, hoping the words I'm imagining won't come from this woman on the doorstep of number ten, its zero with a piece missing. "I have your daughter in my car... Emily?" A tremble of dread makes my voice flutter as the words that will form her reply already sound in my mind.

She pulls the wool tighter and straightens her half-smile of welcome into a line of resignation. Then she says them, the words.

The words.

The words.

"Thomas, your sister died seventeen years ago."

I'd anticipated her saying them. I knew they were coming, and yet they shock me still as I wince at the pain of remembrance. A line of black cars, their roofs rimed with frost, one of them full of flowers. Kicking the zero on the door days later and watching a portion of it break away.

Having said the dreaded words, my mother turns and walks down the hallway, offering me a cup of tea: as matter-of-factly as you like. "Cup of tea?" It's a question, but it's spoken with an implied yes.

I inhale the aroma of freshly baked cake. Coconut. *If I knew you were coming...* I think, not bothering to finish the rest of the lyric as I slowly turn to look at the car and the empty passenger seat.

In a daze I placed a reluctant foot on the doorstep;

eventually the other follows. I fumble behind for the door and hear it thump into its frame. The heavy sound makes me flinch even though it is expected. In the kitchen a kettle rumbles to the boil, its steam rolling around the sweet fragrance of the recently baked cake. The woman has her back to me. She's trying to hide the mopping of her cheek. My eyes glaze over at this point, the hallway turning kaleidoscopic as my shoulders slide down the door. Slumped here on the mat I try to make sense of it all.

The locked portion of my mind has opened. The words she spoke were the key to a door that has been barring me from accessing a room of pain.

I suppose everyone shuts out the pain of their past to some extent. There may be things in the past that they choose to ignore. Or maybe they are completely forgotten; delve a little though and those memories can be found. We tread water on the ocean of our memory and a shallow dive often reveals that which was lost in the silt of time. My ocean obviously runs deep. It runs to places where light usually fails to penetrate.

That light is penetrating now, and it's a penetration of painful clarity.

Like a movie in my head, that night of seventeen years ago rushes back in a sudden torrent of images. We've just moved away from the gun-stand. We are standing astride our bikes at the end of my road,

Sycamore Avenue, looking down the hill in readiness to ride down to Black Bend Bridge. I'm eleven years old. Jack is standing to the left of me, and Martin to the right. The crossbar of my bike rests against my leg, as I lean back and snap the dynamo into contact with the rear tyre. I see Emily pushing her bike up the steep drive to the side of our house. Being only eight years of age it is time for her to be indoors. On lighter nights, if we are playing near to home, mum lets her stay out longer, provided she is with me. But this is the kind of dark evening when devilment comes out to play, and I am with my mates, Jack on the left and Martin on the right, and I have another hour and a half of energy to expend.

After descending the hill at a dangerous speed, we're now standing at the top of the slope that dips into Black Bend Bridge. I'm at the skirt of the hill that holds my memories. We stand in the steelworks shadow, an area of complete darkness. An icy mist floats above the frozen reflection that stretches from curb to curb. We three boys, having flicked dynamo from rubber, are taunting each other, calling one another chicken, clucking, flapping elbows. The hammer pounds steel with a thump that's heavy enough to rattle our ribs. Flame and spark and molten metal glimmers through gaps in the mighty wall of corrugated metal. And the void holds my gaze with its impenetrable menacing blackness.

Hammers thump and my heart pounds.

Jack shoves my left shoulder and calls me chicken. I shove him back and call him the same.

Hammers thump and my heart pounds.

"Chicken," Martin shouts, and so do I, before we again cluck away.

From the rear comes the unmistakable sound of tyre rippling over tarmac. A young girl flies past on her bike.

No lights.

Hammers banging.

Going fast.

Hammers pounding.

Skidding on ice.

Screaming.

Hammers thumping.

The crack of a skull hitting stone, sounding louder in the stillness than any hammer that ever pounded molten steel.

Silence.

Not a sound can be heard, other than the echo of that crack in the void and the sound of my heart pumping in my ears.

It was a young girl called Emily, a young girl who lived at this address, a young girl whose brother is filled with guilt for running away. No! Not running away. Storming up the hill to get help, his muscles burning. Storming up the hill that was more like a mountain to a bicycling eleven year old, my lungs aching as much as if I were swimming from the bottom of a deep ocean.

For all that effort, there was nothing to be done. Emily died the moment her head hit the wall. And the fault is mine, for I knew she was following. The fault is mine, for I ignored the fact rather than have to take her back home, rather than walk all the way up the hill because she didn't have the strength to cycle any further than the church.

Looking up through bleary eyes, seeing my mum walking down the hallway to the spot where I'm crouched on the doormat, I break into wracking sobs, a pain in my heart that's driven by a feeling that Emily died only hours ago.

I sense rather than see Mum crouching next to me. She wraps me with a hug, the wool of the stretched cardigan scratching my tear-soaked cheek.

"Let it out, Son," she says. "Let it out."

From the sound of her voice I can tell that she is crying too. Her tears are quiet, though, not the breath-gasping, shoulder-shuddering, sobs that I don't seem able to bring under control. Her tears have been tempered by time, reduced in intensity by the softening of memory. If not for me, after all this time, her tears would likely be nothing more than an occasional watery-eyed tear of recollection when looking at a photograph or recalling a pleasant event.

Penny theorised that I may have had a traumatic triggering event, that it was locked away, and this is surely it.

"I had a sister," I finally manage to say, as I look into the eyes of a mother who looks much older than the one that has recently sprung into my mind. "She's dead, and it's my fault."

"No, no," she says, squeezing my shoulders into a tighter hug, kissing the top of my head as I slump lower onto the mat. "It was an accident, a terrible accident."

"Have I turned up like this before?" I'm gazing at the floor when I ask, a stream of further questions boiling amid a flood of guilt. Feeling Mum move away from me, I look up to see her heading for the stairs. She turns and sits on the second step and gives me a silent nod of affirmation.

"Yes." The word cracks in her throat and a solitary tear trickles down her cheek. "Every year on the anniversary of Emily's passing"

My mind inserts *death* in place of *passing,* and a fresh well of upset, anger and guilt threatens to rise. I want to ask, *how many years?* But that can wait.

"Every time, Thomas, I ask you where you've been, where you're living, what you're up to with your life, but you never remember…" She looks at me expectantly, her eyes locked on mine as I shake my head. "And you never remember coming back here every January. We always talk for most of the night, me helping you recall the first nineteen years of your life. The next day, we always visit Emily's grave and place flowers. Sometimes you stay for a few days, and I think, I hope that maybe this time... Sometimes you leave the following day. No goodbye or anything. I don't blame you," she blurts in a rush of apology. "I'm certain you don't mean to hurt my feelings. I think that's just the point where you forget, like you lock it away somewhere, the hurt, you know, the guilt and the pain."

A few tears break free and roll down her cheeks. She mops them with a scratch of the faded cardigan. I notice a hole in the right elbow that's been darned with a different shade of green.

"I'm sorry." I want to say more, but right now more words, appropriate words won't come to mind. Right now, all that is in my mind is the past week and the night of my sister's death.

"I know you are, Thomas." Mum manages a shallow smile, and gently nods her acceptance. "You look well. Most years you turn up looking as if you've slept under a bush: freezing and dirty. Always in a dark suit, as if something in the back of your mind has told you to dress for a funeral. I'll make that cup of tea, and..." She pauses midsentence as she pushes herself from the step. "What's the book?"

My fingers press against something hard, and I

look down into my lap. I'm clutching a lilac coloured book. It's just over an inch thick and has a length of similar coloured elastic holding it closed. I don't recall bringing it from the car, but I obviously did. Some part of me must have been desperate to keep a hold of it. "Did you say I went missing when I was nineteen?"

"Nineteen, yes."

Not twenty then. I guessed wrong. I'm twenty-eight, not twenty-nine.

My hand shaking, I lift the journal from my lap and gaze at it. "This is the story of where I've been for the past nine years," I tell her, feeling that I now want to know about the nineteen that preceded them.

CHAPTER

3 2

Before passing any of my new found knowledge to Mum, I tell her that it has all come to me from reading the journal. None of it is from my actual memory, even though much of it now feels as familiar as genuine recollection. Although I'm fairly convinced of its validity, I cannot be certain that it is wholly accurate. I can't even say with absolute certainty that I have personally written the words it contains.

I then give her an edited version, enough to give her a good impression of time place and detail. I tell her about waking up on the streets of London and riding the tube all day before heading to a place called Brookwood. The feeling of sheer terror I felt back then, fresh in my mind from waking on the hill here, only a matter of days back. I tell her about sleeping in a shed that was located in the grounds of a fairly large house, and of feeling so afraid that I didn't sleep for the first two nights. I leave out the incident of preventing a rape, not quite certain if I will tell her at a later date or not. I tell her about spending my days in the library, primarily to keep warm, and that it eventually led to a love of reading. I tell her about being discovered by Mrs Gaskell, and of being invited to work for her in payment of lodgings. The gratitude I felt then comes back to me and fills me with warmth. I tell her of my guitar playing and gigging and gardening for the friends of Mrs Gaskell. Finally I tell her about the woman I apparently love, handing her the photograph. My heart flutters as I speak of her, as I tell about how we met, and the experiences we have shared.

We sit for a moment in silence as I search my mind for more. Mum has listened throughout, not saying a word. She nodded occasionally. She smiled warmly at certain points, and released a sound indicative of wishing to say something at others. Though she didn't speak, I got the impression she wished to, her expression suggesting that she was making mental-notes that would be expressed when I had finished.

"That's everything," I say.

Mum hands Penny's photograph back to me. I realise that the telling came to my mind without effort. It feels like true memory. I also added elements that were not written down. Some of them came fresh from the journal, but many of them swam through my mind like a backdrop, like a film playing quietly on a television in the corner while a conversation was taking place. As we share a moment of contemplative silence, I look at the photograph of Penny and I feel the love I have for her. I truly feel it in every cell of my body.

"Will you do something for me?" I ask Mum, flicking to the back cover of the journal. "Before telling me about my life before I left, will you telephone Penny for me? Here's the number. I would phone her myself, but this remembering feels a little too fragile right now, and I don't want to risk shattering it."

Mum nods, takes the journal from me, and then heads out to the hallway.

Real memory. Real love. I feel like I've found long lost treasure. The sickening sound of my sister's head smashing into the brick wall, seemingly louder than the steel-pounding hammer, comes to mind and causes me to shudder and feel guilt for being pleased to remember a life that she never had a chance to be part of, for enjoying many more years than she ever had, for living and for forgetting and for not deserving.

"Hello," I hear mum say with a tremor of hesitancy. "Am I speaking to a Penny Wilkes? ... My name is Esther Morrison. I – Thomas is my son ... Tom, yes ... Yes, he did say you know him as Gardener ... Yes he is. He came home about an hour ago. Yes, he's safe … Yes, of course. It's 10 Sycamore Avenue, Wincobank, in Sheffield … Yes, South Yorkshire … No need, I have it here, in this journal … Brookwood, yes … My telephone number, certainly…"

Mums voice drifts to the background as I wonder if this will be the time it sticks. Thinking of the research that Penny did, I wonder if I normally remember living in Surrey with Penelope or if this is a one off that has come about purely because of the journal. I guess not. I assume that memory normally comes gradually as I blank out memory of my sister's death. Maybe that is the point that I normally return home, the knowledge of where I've been for the week entirely lost to me. While it's in my head, as painful as it is to do so, I decide to write down the events leading up to Emily's death as well as the way it happened.

I feel for the notebook in my pocket: a record of the time I've spent here. I'm also going to write down what Mum tells me of my life leading up to the point where I first headed south. Hopefully the two halves will mesh together and be large enough to get permanently lodged in my present reality.

CHAPTER

3 3

Mum enters the room carrying a tray of rattling cups on saucers, and a knitted cosy under which there snuggles a fresh pot of tea. She goes back to the kitchen and returns with two plates that each sport a huge slice of coconut cake. "Well, Penny sounds nice," she says, setting the cake onto the table between us.

"She does." It's the only really honest answer I can give right now, despite the comforting warmth that mention of her brings to my heart.

"Seems to really care a lot about you."

"I hope so."

"She's got my telephone number, and address, so hopefully... I haven't told her much about, you know... I thought it best if you tell her, if you remember that is."

The woman is treading so lightly, trying not to break eggshells, she is practically floating. She's no doubt worried that saying too much about my sister's death might crush any reparation that has been made. I completely understand; after all, I'm the eggshell upon which she is walking.

"I can only hope," I say with a grimace, knowing that this scenario has played out before, even if a little differently. At least Penny now knows where I go to during the missing week. If I do forget, she can at least fill me in. "I'm guessing all I've just told you is completely new? I mean, I've never told you anything before about where I've been?"

"No," she says, while pouring the tea. "Nothing."

"When I've turned up in the past, has it always been the same?"

"Always the same date, roughly the same time, but sometimes you're… not in the best of shape, emotionally I mean, not just physically. This is the best I've ever seen you. It's nice."

I can't even begin to think what she's gone through over the past nine years. "There's something I'm struggling to understand. If Emily died when I was eleven, why did I suddenly take off when I was nineteen? Did something happen that…?"

Mum grimaces. "Maybe that's not the best place to begin."

"Alright," I say, before taking a bite of the cake. "This is good," I tell her, mumbling through a mouthful of crumbs. "Better even than Mrs Gaskell's."

Mum chuckles, as if at a private joke. "Sorry. It's one of the things that amused me when you were talking earlier. Saying that the lady has looked out for you and even bakes your favourite cake. Coconut was Emily's favourite. You adopted it as your own after she died. Silly as it sounds, I think things like the cake have stopped you from moving on."

"I'm not sure what you mean."

Mum forms a puzzled expression. "I never know the best way to tell all of this. You'd think I would by now."

"Just start at the beginning," I suggest with a shrug, my pen poised over the open notebook. I don't do shorthand. I'm not expecting to get it all down on paper. I just want enough information to help the memories to stick, a few words that will act as a kind of glue.

"It's hard to know where the beginning is." Mum glances at the sideboard, at the framed photographs that sit upon it. Her gaze lingers for quite a while, a happy smile blossoming on her face and erasing a few of the weary years.

The largest of the pictures shows a close up shot of a man hugging two children. They're dressed in clothes that look suited for keeping out the coldest of weather: padded coats, woollen hats, scarfs, gloves. They each have rosy red cheeks, noses that glow, and smiles of obvious delight sparkling in their eyes.

"We were always such a close family." The smile on Mum's face falters, but then as she appears to look inward, as if reaching for a stored memory, it returns with a greater strength. "It snowed heavy that year… the three of you built an igloo. After warming up a little, the four of us had a picnic inside it."

"That's Emily? And my dad?"

"That's Emily and your dad, and you. I don't recall you and Emily ever bickering. This house was always full of laughter. And music, there was always music. It was such a delight; I miss it terribly. It gladdens me to learn that music has been there for you, Thomas. I'm pleased it's helped to get you through difficult times. It would have pleased your dad, too. I imagine you still play guitar to a high standard?"

With as much humility as I can muster, I nod as a shallow smile creeps onto my lips with the recollection of the gig I performed in The Foundry.

"So you should, the amount of practice you've had. Your dad played the clubs with a small group, singing stuff by bands like Cream and The Eagles. They were good, but not quite good enough to be any more than a cover band. He taught you and Emily to play guitar as soon as you were big enough to hold one. You practiced together, regularly; I guess that might have made you closer than you otherwise might have been."

A flash of memory comes with the disclosure, a

memory of sitting in what I presume to be my bedroom. The recollection is of a young boy and a younger girl sitting on a bed, guitars in hand, playing records and trying to strum along.

"You and Emily used to talk about one day forming your own band. When Emily was eight, when most girls her age were obsessed with Steps and Britney Spears, she followed your fondness for Fleetwood Mac – a fondness that you gained from your dad – and the two of you tried desperately to play tracks that even your dad couldn't manage."

Mum pauses for a moment, glances at the pictures on the sideboard, and then looks at me. "The following January, is when Emily had her accident. You got obsessive about learning to play those songs then. Maybe you felt you were doing it for Emily. Maybe it was just a form of escape. You'd stay up in your room, constantly practicing until your fingers bled. There were two Fleetwood tracks in particular that you'd play over and over, determined to get them perfect…"

"*Big Love*, and *Go Insane*," I offer, knowing without a doubt they are the ones. The memory of a lost and angry, self-punished boy springs to mind, singing lyrics that tell of the pain he was feeling. Lyrics that tell of a house on top of a hill and of looking for love. The song itself may well have meant something different to its creator, but for me it was a rage against life for taking my sister from me. It was an outpouring of regret about not keeping her safe. It was guilt for living when she had died. Through a vague fog of remembering, I get the feeling that I haven't played those two songs in all the while I've gigged in Surrey. Along with the anger and loss, they came to my mind and to my string-strumming fingers with the awakening remembrance of being here, here in the place where that angst was born.

"They're the ones." Mum pauses a moment, various thoughts travelling over her expression. "Strange that you've never remembered before. There was always such pain in your voice when you sang those songs, and anger in the way you played the music. In a little under six months, much to your dad's amazement you had those songs mastered. They couldn't have been played any better by anyone, he reckoned. He wanted you to play with the band, those songs in particular, but you wouldn't, said they were private."

Again, as if looking at distant thoughts, Mum takes a moment. "You'd completely stopped hanging out with your friends, so to get you from your room, we encouraged you to join clubs. You took to karate for some reason, and attacked it with the same amount of conviction and energy as the guitar playing. You continued in that way with everything: with your schoolwork, with driving lessons. You refused to make time for friends throughout, but you spent plenty of time with your dad. We often talked about university, your grades being so good that you could have had your pick, but although you succeeded in everything you did, you tackled them with no real sense of direction. It was almost as if you were looking for something to beat you, instead of you beating it. I think you were just looking for an excuse to give up, to stop trying. Eventually something came along that did beat you, something you couldn't practise into submission."

It takes me a moment to realise that Mum has stopped talking. I am too occupied with scribbling down notes and taking in the memories that come with her words. I look up to see a pained expression on her face, and as her eyes meet mine she releases a heavy sigh.

"What?" I asked.

She shakes her head slightly, as if demonstrating a reluctance to go on. "In the September before you turned nineteen, your dad passed away." Tears trickle down her cheeks. "Cancer. He'd been fighting it for just over a year. We didn't tell you, because... we decided you were already suffering enough... we should have told you. After the funeral you stayed in your room. Days would go by when I hardly saw you. I think you blamed me, for not telling. Maybe you blamed us both, I don't know, but I was the only one here for you to put the blame on.

"Things really went down hill then. You had your excuse to give up fighting. You rarely bathed. You ate sporadically. You stopped playing music and listening to music. You stopped attending karate. You stopped doing anything. The doctor came to see you. He prescribed anti-depressants and counselling. You refused both. You just wanted to be left alone. So I left you alone. I tried to avoid being in the same room, because that's what you obviously wanted. I wouldn't even enter the kitchen when you came down to grab a bite to eat, though I always went in after to see what you had taken so I could replace the things you liked. I got very efficient at making coconut cake," she says with a huff of pained amusement.

"One evening – around six – I realised that I'd not seen or heard you for the entire day. As quiet as you were, I'd listen out for little sounds: the creak of a floorboard, the flush of the toilet, the running of a tap. Thinking the worst, I checked your room and discovered that you weren't there. I didn't know if you'd been gone for the entire day, or if you'd just gone out mere moments ago. Maybe a click of the catch on the backdoor had alerted me but not registered for a few moments. A small part of me was pleased, despite the underlying anxiety, thinking that perhaps you'd gone for a walk, and that maybe things would now begin to get better. Late that night, when you hadn't come back home, I realised – how I could have forgotten I don't know, too distracted I suppose – I realised that it was the anniversary of Emily's death.

"In the early hours of the morning, I walked down the hill to that bridge. Someone, I guessed you, had placed flowers by the wall. I walked around the area for two hours, hoping to find you. I went home, hoping you'd returned. You hadn't.

"It was a year to the day when I saw you next. You stood on the step and told me that you had my daughter in your car. My reaction wasn't as calm as it was today. I was angry. I thought you were playing some sort of cruel joke. When the truth dawned on you and you broke down in tears, I realised that you had genuinely forgotten. I told you then, pretty much all I have told you just now."

"I'm sorry… I – I don't know why…"

"I know you are, Thomas. Believe me, I don't blame you. That first year you were missing was very painful; I was constantly wondering what had become of you. It was especially difficult when you went away again, leaving me none-the-wiser in regard to your whereabouts. It has got easier over time, and knowing that you had no memory of Emily and her death made me realise that you hadn't gone away like that just to punish me. As hard as it was to take, knowing that at least gave me a little comfort. And now, knowing that you have been living a full and happy life, I couldn't be any happier."

Mum's tears flow afresh, but they seem to be tears diluted with a measure of joy and hope. I move to join her on the sofa and, feeling a little like a stranger pretending to be her son, take her hands in mine. "I can't imagine the pain I've put you through," I tell her, "but I am going to do my utmost to remember and to put things right. I do have to ask something, though: did you ever try to find me?"

She nods slowly and forces a reassuring smile. "After waiting twenty-four hours, I contacted the police. I would have done so sooner, but I thought you had to wait that long; you don't. They weren't overly concerned, because of you being nineteen. They asked if you had any money. I checked your room and found two recent cash-point receipts, each showing a withdrawal amount of one hundred and twenty pounds. I hadn't even been aware of you leaving the house. They said the cash withdrawals demonstrated rational thought with an element of planning. In answering their questions, I told them honestly that we hadn't got along for months, ever since your dad had passed away. They said the placement of the flowers was perhaps a sign of saying goodbye, that you'd likely gone somewhere to make a fresh start. You weren't classed as high-risk. They filed a report labelling you as *absent*, not as *missing*. They advised me to get in touch with friends and ask if they knew anything. You'd shunned any friends years ago, but I asked everyone I could think of all the same. They helped as best they could, but all enquiries led to nothing. For the first couple of years, when you turned up and then left, I asked if anyone had seen you walking around in the area. Nobody ever had. Maybe you avoided being seen, by anyone. I don't know. I thought someone might see you, recognise you, but no. Maybe you haven't explored around here in the past. Do you think maybe you only did that because of the book?"

"It's possible, I suppose. You said I generally don't look as clean and healthy when I turn up on your doorstep. Perhaps I do sometimes sleep under a bush." I think back to the seedy hotel with the grubby sheets. "Or worse."

Mum frowns, slightly, perhaps wondering what could be worse that sleeping under a bush.

"Over time, you have matured, filled out, too, so perhaps people around here wouldn't recognise you if they did see you. I know sometimes I see someone I think I recognise from my past, and I give them that look, you know, the kind that says: *hello, do I know you?* If that look isn't returned, I just think I must be mistaken and move on. Over time, I suppose people forget too. You were always at the front of my mind, but you cut people out of your life before you'd even become a teen, so I guess… people move away, get on with their own lives. Looking out for you would be the last thing on their minds. I suppose people look without seeing too. The old friends asked about you less and less, until eventually they stopped asking altogether.

"It was pretty much the same with the police," she said, shrugging her shoulders. "In truth they probably did more than I remember. It was all a kind of frantic haze. I was still mourning the loss of your dad, which made it hard for me to do all that I might have done. I just felt like I was being mollified and given the brush-off."

"Can't have been easy," I say, thinking the words more than inadequate, but not really having anything to put in their place.

"After a few months I contacted a private investigator. He was a nice man. Kind. Understanding. Sympathetic. He told me that without a solitary lead, it was nigh on impossible to find someone who didn't wish to be found, that apart from not being likely to succeed, such a search could prove very expensive. He gave me some frightening statistics to illustrate his point. Apparently the number of missing reported each year in the UK is over two hundred thousand, around one person every two minutes, but only around ten a week are found. He told me that almost half of missing adults that are found don't want to make contact with the people that are looking for them. Of the ones he'd found in the past, he claimed they were fleeing from something – either in reality or in their own minds. He convinced me that many missing people are missing because they want to be; they use false names, have cash-in-hand jobs, live in hostels or short lets or squats… or lodge with helpful old ladies."

I sense a hint of bitterness in her tone. I can't really blame her, knowing I've done many of the things on her list. "I wasn't trying to avoid being found, I just didn't know where to start. I just did what I had to do to survive. maybe I could have gone to the police, but I was afraid. I had a strong feeling that I'd done something wrong, like rape or murder, or… It just… as time went on, it was just easier to live the way I was doing."

Mum nods her understanding and gives my hand a gentle pat before then giving it a squeeze of reassurance. "Like I said, it got easier with each passing year for me too. That investigator's words often came to mind, about many missing people not actually being missing, but just not wanting to be found. I won't lie; when you came home each year, I actually thought you probably did know where you'd been living, but that you just didn't want me to know. That was hard to accept, but it took some of the worry away, and I just waited for this yearly visit. As stressful as it is, at least I get to see you; I get to know you're still alive and well. And now," she says, acknowledging the lilac journal with a tip of her head. "I feel that you were telling me the truth."

CHAPTER

3 4

Gripping the lilac journal and the black notebook as if they are interconnected lifelines, I enter the bedroom that I slept in up to the age of nineteen. It's the small box-room. Situated at the front of the house, it looks onto the vast landscape that stretches out from the skirt of the hill. I remember being in this room as a child. I remember being lulled to sleep by the distant thump of hammers pounding steel. I remember looking at the motorway at night, and marvelling at the string of lights that stretched along its length from side to side.

The room contains a single bed that has been neatly dressed. It looks crisp and white and inviting. By the window stands a small wardrobe, to the side of that a chest of drawers upon which sits a stereo with a turntable, a collection of vinyl LPs racked between it and the wardrobe's side. Above the stereo a shelf strains under a weight of trophies, most of them for karate, some for swimming, all of them sporting my name: Thomas Morrison. Two posters are blue-tacked to the wall above the bed. One of them shows Stevie Nicks and Lindsey Buckingham on stage, the other Aerosmith.

On a stand by the side of the bed is a guitar that very much resembles the Tanglewood I have back at Penny's. The dark-wood body no doubt shouted something into my mind when I saw it in the shop. It was all in there, all along: the knowledge of everything to do with my life, in storage, in a locked room, just as Penny's research suggested. I pick up the guitar and give the strings a gentle strum. It's out of tune, but it hasn't simply sat here waiting for my return: there's not a speck of dust on it. In fact, there's not a speck of dust in the entire room. I inhale the bedding and its freshly laundered aroma. I'm guessing the bed has been made today because laundry fragrance soon dissipates. Of course it has, she was expecting me.

I feel the sting of tears building in my eyes, as I suddenly recall playing guitar with Emily in this very room, as I picture Dad popping his head around the door and giving us a thumbs-up and a massive smile. A mix of sadness and happiness swirls through my gut and chest, as the far past and the recent past blend in my mind.

Tomorrow I will go and visit the grave of both Emily and Dad with my mum. It's something I need to do, apparently something we've always done, but a part of me is afraid that it might be the trigger that will push me into wanting to forget. That's not quite right, though: I don't believe I ever wanted to forget; it seems to me that I had to forget.

Memories continue to trickle into my mind. They come to me in a random order – not following a linear timeline – with something of one triggering the next. Like a reservoir filling up, the memories seemingly settle in order of importance: some like silt settling to the bottom, accessible but needing a little work in order to be viewed, others floating on the surface, visibly rippling and catching sparks of brilliant sunlight.

Picking up the notebook, using the lilac journal as a kind of desk upon my lap, afraid of separating them, I make a start on writing anything down that comes to mind. I have no way of knowing if they are genuine memories, for now, but I need to record them, just in case. If I write them down, I can ask Mum for confirmation. I doubt that I have ever remembered my life in Surrey while sitting in this room. I'm guessing I have never remembered both parts of my life at the same time.

Hopefully, the two will now mesh.

Hopefully, I am on the cusp of the point where I can finally move on with my life.

Maybe now the yin and yang of my life will merge into one.

Maybe now I will become whole.

CHAPTER

3 5

March has come around quickly and accelerated to this day with a flurry of last minute organisation. I throw Penny a smile of appreciation as she begins removing cling-film protection from the buffet we have spent all day preparing.

"You okay?" she mouths, before reflecting my smile.

Nodding that I am, I then smile again, more broadly, as she casts a quick eye over our efforts. I don't seem able to take my eyes away from her, this woman who stole my heart and put something bigger and more mysterious in its place. As bad as my failed memory has been, without it I would never have met Penny. I don't really believe in spirits and ghosts and such, but I like to think that somehow Emily encouraged me to get onto that train and go to London. I like to think that my departed sister led me to the woman of my destiny.

I am okay. I seem to be holding onto the things I

have learned of my past. It's not a complete account, but whose memory is totally complete? And how much can memory be trusted anyway? There are some things I don't want to remember, like what truly happened when I was chasing the guy on the towpath. And anyway, doesn't each and every one of us forget certain events or restructure the way in which they unfolded? When telling someone about something we have done, don't we all embellish if the account paints us as the hero, or redact if the account is something in which the part we played brings us shame? Do we not over time come to believe those altered accounts and fix them to some form of false permanency in our minds? And once a false memory is fixed, how would we know it to be false without someone to corroborate or deny?

I'm trying my best is all I can say. There's a road of repair to travel. Something seems to be troubling Penny, too, but we're together and we'll help each other. Now I'm aware of their existence on a day-to-day basis, I miss my sister and my dad terribly. To me it is as if they died only a few months ago. It feels raw, and sometimes I cry. I'm lucky though, for I have the support of people that love me.

The thought of people loving me makes me chuckle, as not for the first, second or even third time this night, Pauline throws me a scowl of annoyance that she struggles to maintain as friends she has come to know over the years turn up and congratulate her on reaching ninety years of age.

"Take no notice," Penny says, approaching from behind and throwing her arms around me. "She's loving every minute of it. Look how she's grinning when looking anywhere other than your direction."

Penny's not telling me anything I hadn't already deduced. My old friend is just getting a measure of enjoyment out of making me suffer for organising a surprise party in her honour. When she glances back and sees me smirking, she has a quick look to see if anyone is looking at her. Deciding that nobody is, she returns my smile and mouths a big *thank you*, before stroking a solitary finger under each eye.

"Nice to see her and my mum getting along," I say to Penny, as Mum throws me a little wave and then turns to continue chatting with Pauline. "I doubt they've had a minute without talking since Mum first arrived."

"It's hardly surprising." Penny slinks her way around me and begins to sway her hips to the rhythm of the music. She looks into my eyes and places her hands on my shoulders. "They've got plenty of notes to swap."

Guilt still washes over me when I think about what I've put other people through. I slip into detachment, and right now it's like Penny is dancing with a statue as an element of dread reminds me that the memories might once more escape my grasp. It's in the good moments that I fear it the most. I told Penny about Nicky, how I met her and befriended her at the pub up in Sheffield, assuring her that nothing untoward happened. I contacted Nicky the day I got back to Surrey, telephoning her with Penny by my side. I needed to let her know I was safely back home with my memory somewhat restored. She was pleased for me, but I'm certain I detected a note of disappointment in her tone. I can't help but wonder what would have happened between Nicky and me were it not for the journal. I can't help but wonder if I've transgressed in earlier disappearances.

"I'm sorry," I tell Penny, my voice cracking a little.

"I know you are. You've told me often enough. It's time to move forward, Tom. Stop looking back. Cheer up and shut up," she commands with a grin as she places her hand over my mouth, "and just dance with me will you?" Her nose scrunches in the cute way I love as she says words that bring a song to my mind.

Pauline wasn't the only one to be greeted with a surprise tonight, and I glance over at where my guitar awaits my performance, where it sits on the small stage by the disk jockey's decks. I should cheer up. My memories are sticking, and so they should; I read the notebook every day. There'll be no angry songs tonight, no songs full of angst and reflective sadness. Inspired by Penny's words, as I look into her sparkling eyes and see my future, I know exactly what the first song of the night is going to be.

The music and our current dance come to a close. I wave to the DJ to let him know I'm ready, my mood in just the right place.

"A little live music, now folks," says the DJ, his voice muffled from holding the mike too close. "Put your hands together, please, for our local celebrity, Tom Gardener."

To a smattering of applause I head for the stage, wondering whether or not to keep Gardener as a stage name. It's who I'm known as for my music, after all; It's a name I've gone by for the past nine years of my life, and a key to many memories. I take off my favourite leather jacket and place it over the back of a chair, checking that the box containing a diamond ring is still safely secreted in the inner pocket. There is going to be no more holding back, though I have yet to decide on whether to ask Penny to marry me tonight, among all our friends, or wait until a month's time when we're in Barcelona for Penny's twenty-sixth. *I'll decide later.* Picking up the guitar, I turn on the amp and give the strings a bit of final tuning.

I look around the room, pleased that I know every face looking back at me. "Thanks for coming everyone." I chuckle as even that comment gets a smattering of applause. "Happy birthday, Pauline," I say with a wink. "Sorry... Mrs Gaskell. She'll kill me for that you know. Witnesses," I say, pointing around the room, before pointing at Pauline who's grinning and shaking her head at me.

Laughter ripples around the room as Pauline waves a fist, then turns and says something to my mum that makes her laugh.

"You might know this number," I tell the room. "It's one I've not played to an audience before. It was quite big in the charts last year, and I really like it." *I like all songs where the lyrics mean something personal to me,* and this one does: because of Penny's recent words, it marks this night. I break into the opening chords, a melody that is upbeat and inspires an essence of dance and enjoyment. "It's by a band called 'Walk The Moon', called 'Shut Up and Dance'… Please do."

Kaitlyn whoops and drags Penny to the dance floor as I break into the opening lines with an enthusiasm that's inspired by my own situation. "I LOVE THIS TUNE!" Kaitlyn shouts, elevating my mood, as Penny blows me a smacker of a kiss with both hands.

Yes, I say to myself with a feeling of satisfaction. Tonight may be the night I ask Penny to marry me.

Thank you for reading this novel. I hope you found it an enjoyable read. It would be great if you could spare a moment to give a rating on Amazon or Goodreads, or both. If you have a little extra time to spare, and feel inclined to do so, a review to let other readers know what you thought would be fantastic and much appreciated. Your point of view really does make a difference.

Printed in Great Britain
by Amazon